HIGH SCHOOL BITES

HEATHER

EIGHTH GRADE BITES

THE CHRONICLES OF VLADIMIR TOD · BOOK 1

FIRST KILL

THE SLAYER CHRONICLES · BOOK 1

together in one volume

speak

An Imprint of Penguin Group (USA) Inc.

THE CHRONICLES OF Vladimir Tod

EIGHTH GRADE BITES

SPEAK
Published by the Penguin Group
Penguin Group (USA) Inc., 345 Hudson Street, New York, New York 10014, U.S.A.
Penguin Group (Canada), 90 Eglinton Avenue East, Suite 700, Toronto, Ontario, Canada M4P 2Y3
(a division of Pearson Penguin Canada Inc.)
Penguin Books Ltd, 80 Strand, London WC2R 0RL, England
Penguin Ireland, 25 St Stephen's Green, Dublin 2, Ireland (a division of Penguin Books Ltd)
Penguin Group (Australia), 250 Camberwell Road, Camberwell, Victoria 3124, Australia
(a division of Pearson Australia Group Pty Ltd)
Penguin Books India Pvt Ltd, 11 Community Centre, Panchsheel Park, New Delhi – 110 017, India
Penguin Group (NZ), 67 Apollo Drive, Rosedale, Auckland 0632, New Zealand
(a division of Pearson New Zealand Ltd.)
Penguin Books (South Africa) (Pty) Ltd, 24 Sturdee Avenue, Rosebank, Johannesburg 2196, South Africa

Penguin Books Ltd, Registered Offices: 80 Strand, London WC2R 0RL, England

First published in the United States of America by Dutton Children's Books,
a division of Penguin Group (USA) Inc., 2007
Published by Speak, an imprint of Penguin Group (USA) Inc., 2008
This bindup edition published by Speak, an imprint of Penguin Group (USA) Inc., 2012

1 3 5 7 9 10 8 6 4 2

Copyright © Heather Brewer, 2007
All rights reserved

CIP Data is available.

This edition ISBN 978-0-14-242460-5

Printed in the United States of America

ALWAYS LEARNING

PEARSON

▼ ▼ ▼

To my husband, Paul—Stephen King knows why.
And to every unpopular kid in
small-town America.

ACKNOWLEDGMENTS

First and foremost, I'd like to thank my wonderful editor, Maureen Sullivan, and everyone else at Dutton, as well as my fabulous agent, Michael Bourret, for their direction, wisdom, assistance, and guidance. Collectively, you've changed my life in ways you may never know.

Many thanks to Jackie Kessler and Dawn Vanniman for being faithful readers, wonderful friends, and much-needed critics. Special thanks should be given to Jacob Elwart and Katelyn Vanniman for loving this book from the start. Many thanks to all of my minions—you know who you are. Thanks should also be expressed to the Pepsi-Cola Company for supplying me with enough caffeine to finish the book; to Ardyn—who really started this whole mess in the first place; and to Jacob and Alexandria—thanks for not popping my bubble *too* often.

Most important, thanks to the person holding this book right now. You have no idea how much you mean to me (or Vlad).

Finally, words alone cannot express the thanks I owe to Paul Brewer, my husband, for his encouragement and assistance. You knew I could do it before I had any clue. Thank you.

Contents

The Chronicles of Vladimir Tod

EIGHTH GRADE BITES

1
WHERE'S THE BOY?

A TREE BRANCH SLAPPED JOHN CRAIG across the face, scraping his skin, but he kept on running and ignored the stabbing of pine needles on his bare feet. He could hear the man's footsteps behind him, echoing his own.

The man was getting closer.

A fallen branch grabbed John's ankle and he fell forward. Time slowed to a crawl as his face neared the leaf-covered ground. Cold air whipped across his skin. His heart drummed in his ears. The man's pace quickened, and just as John's cheek smacked against the earth, the stranger grabbed a fistful of John's hair and pulled his head back. John screeched, "What do you want from me?" but his attacker didn't answer.

John swung his arms behind him to knock the man down, but his hands were caught effortlessly in the air and bound behind him. A hand, gloved in shiny black leather, entered his field of vision, clutching a torn page from the *Bathory Gazette*.

John's head jerked back as the man gave his hair a violent tug and growled, "Where is he?"

At the center of the paper was the grainy image of a thirteen-year-old boy John knew well. The boy was surrounded by several of his peers and a teacher, but looked nervous, awkward. At the bottom of the photo, a caption read: *Left to right: Kelly Anbrock, Carrie Anderson, Henry McMillan, teacher John Craig, Vladimir Tod, Edgar Poe, Mike Brennan.* At the top was a bold title: **Debate Team Sure to Win at Regionals!**

Tears coated John's cheeks and he shook his head, refusing to answer.

Something warm and slick ran down John's forehead. Through red-tinted glass, he looked at the forest around them. He screamed for help until his lungs burned, but help wouldn't come.

"Where's the boy? Where's Vlad?"

John wriggled. The man's face was near his. Cold breath beat down on the back of his neck, and something sharp grazed against his skin.

"Tell me or die."

John opened his mouth to speak, but it was too late for lies. The man bit down. Fangs popped through John's skin, cutting deep into his neck.

2
HALLOWEEN

VLAD TURNED TO THE SIDE, admiring his image in the mirror with a smirk. Henry was going to lose it when he saw Vlad's costume. They hadn't discussed what they were dressing up as, but the pathetic black nylon cape and plastic fangs that Vlad had picked up at the Stop & Shop last weekend were sure to be the running gag of the evening between them. He brushed his black hair from his eyes and slipped the plastic teeth into his mouth. They fit perfectly over his own fangs, which were protruding slightly, despite his large dinner.

Not an hour before, Aunt Nelly had warmed two sizable steaks until the blood dripped from the raw meat. He'd restrained himself from picking up the steaks with his bare hands and ripping into them, but only because Aunt Nelly insisted on manners. So even though it agonized him to do so, he took his time, cutting the steaks into medium-size bites and sucking the juices into his hungry mouth before dropping the dry, tasteless meat onto his plate.

He pulled the fake teeth out of his mouth and examined the sharp points of his fangs. "Aunt Nelly, you'd better get a snack pack ready."

"But you just ate," came a lilting voice from the bottom of the stairs. "Oh well, better safe than sorry, I suppose. What time will Henry be here?"

"Any minute." Satisfied with his costume, Vlad turned from the mirror. The old floorboards creaked beneath his sneakers. He kissed his fingers and pressed them to the frame on his dresser. In the photo, his mother was poised on the edge of an old Victorian chaise, with his father standing behind her, his pale hands on her shoulders. They were smiling at the camera, and Vlad found himself smiling back at them. He opened the top drawer and stuffed ten dollars from his secret box into his pocket. Partying with Henry had taught him one thing above all else: be prepared.

Vlad left his bedroom and made his way down the stairs. Aunt Nelly stood at the bottom, holding up a plastic container covered with Saran Wrap. He could see the deep red, slushy contents through the wrap and licked his lips. "Did you microwave it? It's better warm."

"It's warm enough." She handed it to him and widened her eyes in disgust as he bit through the Saran Wrap and slurped. "Use a spoon! You'll get it all over the rug and I just had it cleaned. Between that rug and your T-shirts, the dry cleaner thinks we're either accident-prone or ax murderers. And take it easy on the snack packs tonight, Mr. Midnight Feeder. There are only two left. I'd better bring some more blood bags from the hospital tonight and fix up enough for the rest of the week."

"Could you get O positive this time? That's my favorite." She nodded and he smiled, brushing past her to the kitchen. He was spooning a big, sweet glob of half-frozen blood into his mouth when the doorbell rang. With a hurried swallow, he dropped the empty container into the biohazard box beneath the sink and popped the plastic fangs over his shrinking canines. With careful steps, he snuck over to the wall just to the right of the archway and peeked over at the front door, where his aunt was greeting Henry with a hug.

Vlad jumped out from behind the separating wall and held his cheap cape out with both arms. "I vant to suck your blood!"

Henry doubled over, roaring with laughter. When he straightened, he slapped Vlad on the shoulder. "That's a sweet costume. Check me out. You'll just die." Henry placed his fists on his hips in a pseudo-Superman pose, and when he turned his head, Vlad's jaw dropped at the sight of two small holes on Henry's neck.

"No way." He stepped closer to inspect Henry's bite marks. They were flawless. Vlad had only seen one actual vampire bite on a human before, and Henry's handiwork was very close to the real thing. "What did you use?"

"Silly Putty and raspberry jam."

"Seedless?"

"Well, duh. Can't have seeds in my wound. Might get infected."

Aunt Nelly regarded Vlad with a concerned glance over the top of her glasses. "Did you get enough to eat?"

Vlad nodded, stuffed a tube of his sunscreen into his pocket, and opened the door. "Party's over at midnight."

Nelly held out her hand. "You won't need that. I want you home by eleven."

"Eleven?" At times, Nelly could be ridiculously overprotective. Vlad rolled his eyes and dug the tube back out, slapping it into Nelly's hand. "But no one else will be leaving early, and besides, at midnight there's supposed to be some big surprise."

Nelly looked at Henry for confirmation. He nodded enthusiastically. "We can't miss it."

"Well…" She bit her lip in contemplation, and after what seemed like an eternity, she sighed. "All right, but stick together, and if you get hungry, give me a call on my cell. I'll be at Deb's until late."

Henry nudged Vlad with his elbow. "Matthew called me earlier, said Meredith will be there."

Vlad shot him a look that screamed "shut up," and they bounded out the door, vampire and victim. Nelly called after them, "Be careful, boys."

Other than the fake wound, Henry was dressed as he normally was, with a pair of ratty-looking sneakers on his feet. He gave Vlad a sly glance. "Big thing at midnight, huh?"

Vlad shrugged and adjusted the cape around his shoulders. "I'm a creature of the night, for God's sake. And she wants me home by eleven? I don't think so. Why doesn't she just follow me to the party and kiss me good-bye?"

"Hey, don't knock it. If it weren't for Nelly, you'd never get kissed."

Vlad slowed his steps. "Like you've got room to talk."

Henry shrugged. "I've kissed plenty of girls."

"I'm not talking about your mom, dork." They turned down Elm, and at the end of the street, Vlad could see cars stopping in front of Matthew's house. A blur of people moved from vehicle to house, and Vlad felt a twinge of nervousness settle into his muscles. The headlights from one of the cars that had been in front of Matthew's house turned toward them, blinding Vlad temporarily.

Henry had shoved his hands into his front pockets and was walking with his attention keenly focused on the sidewalk. "Neither am I. I'm talking about girls like Carrie Anderson and Stephanie Brawn."

"Stephanie will kiss anyone."

"Yeah. I know." Henry's smile returned. "Her sister's cute, though."

Vlad raised an eyebrow, half chuckling. "Dude, that's gross. She just turned twelve."

"So?" Henry grinned broadly.

"So you'll be fourteen in like two months. It's gross." Vlad shook his head and looked down at his right shoe, where his toe was poking through a tear.

Impossibly, Henry's grin broadened. "She's nice."

"Whether or not a girl will kiss you isn't a measure of how nice she is." Ahead, Vlad could see the hint of a soft blue sweater and angel wings disappearing into Matthew's front door. Meredith. He'd overheard her in third period yesterday gushing over what she planned to wear. It was that moment that he'd decided to accept the invitation to the party, last-minute or not.

"So what is, Einstein?"

Vlad stopped in his tracks. Henry had stopped walking as well and tilted his head with a curious gleam in his eye. Vlad nodded and said, "Girls that make out in the back of the band room aren't nice."

"I never told you it was the band room." Henry furrowed his brow and grabbed Vlad's shoulder for a second, lowering his voice so eavesdroppers couldn't hear. "Dude, don't do that freaky mind-reading stuff. I hate that."

Vlad shrugged and kept walking.

Henry nudged Vlad with his elbow and gestured to a group of three trick-or-treaters in front of them with a nod. "Want some candy?"

"I shouldn't. Nelly's still ticked about last year." Vlad shoved his hands in his pockets and looked from his best friend to the kids on the sidewalk. "You know, those kids told their parents they were attacked by a vampire. And that idiot Officer Thompson started asking my aunt all sorts of questions. If people find out about me, about what I am ..."

"Oh, come on." Henry had stepped in front of him, partially blocking Vlad's view of the receding fourth graders. Two were dressed as superheroes of some sort. The third wore the same cape that Vlad had on. "It'll be funny. Besides, if you don't do it ... I'm totally telling Meredith that you like her." Henry turned away and wrapped his arms around himself, making kissing sounds.

Vlad seethed. "Dude! Not cool!"

The grin on Henry's face made it clear that he wasn't about to let a good gag go without a fight. With a shaking head, Vlad relented. "If we get caught you owe me big-time."

Henry beamed. "And I did that without any of the special powers normally associated with best friends of the undead."

Henry stepped to the side and Vlad moved past him, ducking through the tall bushes that lined the sidewalk. Vlad ran as quietly as he could until he stood half a block ahead of his costumed victims. After shimmying up an old oak tree, the bark rough on his hands as he climbed, Vlad scooted out onto a long, thick branch and waited for the fourth graders while Henry stayed in the bushes. He could feel Henry's approving eyes on him and had to stifle a chuckle.

As the superheroes and their vampire comrade approached the tree Vlad was perched in, their fingers clutching pillowcases filled with sugary treats. Vlad popped the plastic fangs out and stuffed them in his front pocket. He let his imagination wander a bit, through rivers of blood and hunger that screamed to be satiated. Touching the tip of his tongue to his newly exposed fangs, he leaned forward until his feet slipped from the branch. Wind brushed his hair back from his face as he descended and then, with a flicker of concentration, Vlad willed his body forward. Arms outstretched, his fangs exposed, his throat releasing a low, guttural growl, he floated closer to the boys until he was just above their heads, and screamed.

The superheroes dropped their pillowcases and bolted in a blur of capes and shrieking terror. The vampire was left behind, staring up at Vlad in a horrified moment that dragged on forever. Vlad screamed again and so did the boy, finally relinquishing his hold on the bag. He was frozen to the spot. Vlad wondered if he would ever run away.

Vlad could hear the boy's heart pounding against his ribs, a loud thunder echoing through his mind. He heard the whoosh of rushing blood and felt the boy's tightened panic in his own chest. Then, in a blink, Vlad saw himself floating down, cheap plastic cape fluttering behind him, bright, sharp fangs shining in the streetlight.

The urge to wet his pants was undeniable, but what would Mark and Todd think if they saw? But then why should he care what they thought. They were mean jerks and had run away without him. And when they found out he was dead the next day, they'd feel awful and deserved to.

Vlad blinked again, squeezing his eyes tight and opening them once more. His feet came to rest on the ground in front of the boy. He'd read the little vampire's thoughts without even trying. Vlad whispered, "You should get home now," which seemed to be the magic words required to release the boy's feet from where they'd been cemented into the sidewalk. The boy ran past him, the pitter-patter of his steps quieting as he shrank down the street in the direction his companions had gone.

Henry burst from the bushes, cackling wildly, and snatched one of the fallen pillowcases from the pavement. "Did you see his face? I thought he was going to wet himself." He dug out a pack of peanut-butter cups and tore open the orange wrapper. Stuffing one of the cups into his mouth, he held the other out to Vlad.

Vlad lifted the sweet chocolate to his lips and bit, his fangs shrinking back in his moment of confusion. The candy melted in his mouth, but he found little pleasure in it.

Henry ran ahead, calling over his shoulder for Vlad to hurry. Vlad picked up the little vampire's bag and ran to catch up just as Henry was stepping onto the porch of Matthew's house. Music was blaring from the open door, and flecks of colored lights hit the porch from inside. Matthew's mom greeted them with laughter. "Well, come on in, you evil dudes! The party's started and it's totally rockin'!"

Vlad and Henry exchanged looks. It was both sad and annoying when adults tried to act cool. Without comment, they walked inside. The living-room furniture had been pushed back against the walls, and a large, mirrored disco ball was suspended from the ceiling. Bursts of fog occasionally covered the floor with a hiss. Vlad counted twenty of his schoolmates before he gave up trying to figure out how many were there, but not before he noticed Meredith standing near the punch bowl at the opposite end of the room, giggling with several of her girlfriends.

Henry nudged him and said something, but Vlad couldn't hear over the loud music, so he nodded and watched as Henry was swallowed by the crowd. Left to his own devices, Vlad took an empty spot on the end of the couch and waited for Henry to return. Bill Jensen and Tom Gaiber were moving toward the front door. Vlad shrank into his seat, hoping they wouldn't notice him. Bill looked straight at him and pulled on Tom's sleeve until Tom nearly fell over on top of Vlad. "Oh my God, check this geek out."

Tom guffawed. "Nice costume, goth boy."

Vlad glared and turned away. "Nice breath, loser."

Matthew's mom was standing near the door, watching the situation with pity-filled eyes. Vlad wished she'd look away, but she continued to stare as the skinny, pale, unpopular boy was picked on. He hoped she'd have enough sense not to try to comfort him after they'd gone, or worse, before. To Vlad's relief, Bill and Tom started moving out the door. Then, to rub salt in the wound, Bill yelled as loud as he could, "Bite me!"

A hot flash shot through Vlad's insides, and in that moment, he was prepared to oblige. He could feel his incisors lengthening, pushing his plastic fangs down, away from his gums. Clamping his mouth shut, he waited a moment to be certain Bill and Tom had gone, and then stepped out onto the porch and stretched, knowing it would take a few minutes to calm his hunger.

The cool quiet of the wraparound porch was a much-welcome distraction from the party. Bill and Tom's taunts had left him with that uncomfortable, hollow sensation for which the only known cure was a few hours at home, battling evildoers for the fate of the earth. People could say what they wanted about video games contributing to the delinquency of minors, but Vlad was sure that if Bill and Tom spent more time playing PlayStation, they'd spend far less taunting him.

He flopped down on the porch swing and listened to the music pouring out the front door. He was kidding himself if he thought he'd be able to ask Meredith to the dance. Girls like Meredith Brookstone didn't date boys like Vladimir Tod.

Besides, the hickeys would be a nightmare.

His fangs shrank back, and as he stood, he heard Meredith's voice, sweet and giggly, coming through the open kitchen window. "Are you asking me out?"

Vlad's heart sank into his stomach, then squeezed its way down his leg and popped out of the hole in his shoe, where it struck the floor and broke. That was what it felt like anyway.

He snuck over to the window and, holding his breath, peeked inside.

Henry was sitting on the kitchen counter, his sneakers dangling. He leaned forward and whispered to Meredith, whose soft brown hair was swept behind each ear. Her lips were pursed in a pout while she listened. Vlad tried not to jump to conclusions, but the sight of Henry's lips moving just inches from Meredith's pretty ear was enough to send his mood plummeting to levels of jealousy he'd not been aware he was capable of experiencing.

Henry glanced up at the window. Vlad ducked, but it was too late—he'd been seen. Moments later Henry was on the porch. "That wasn't what it looked like."

Vlad tried to play it cool, to grasp the last remaining thread of dignity he had and come off uncaring and nonchalant. Instead, his voice cracked and a lump formed in his throat. "This was a mistake. Maybe I should just go home."

"Already? What about Meredith?"

Vlad hurried ahead, shrugging as he descended the porch steps. "It looked to me like she was in good hands."

Henry followed, stopping Vlad with a hand on his shoulder. "You've got it all wrong. I was trying to hook you up for the dance." He looked at Vlad. "You believe me, don't you?"

Sure, he believed Henry. But it was hard to ignore the fact that Henry was probably the most crushed-on guy at Bathory Junior High. At times, the wistful sighs from interested girls as they passed in the hall were deafening. Still...this was Henry. If Vlad could trust anyone, it was him.

Vlad managed a smile. "Of course I do." He continued down the steps with Henry following close behind.

Henry said, "Did you hear about Mr. Craig?"

"What, is he going to be out sick for another week? I don't think I can handle any more of Snelgrove's pop quizzes."

Henry slowed his steps. "People are saying he's been declared missing."

"No way." Vlad stopped walking for a moment and let it sink in. With concentrated effort, he moved forward and tried to erase the possibilities from his mind. "Does anybody know anything?"

Henry had lost the pillowcase, but his front pockets were bulging with candy. "Not really. They say he just up and disappeared."

"Weird."

"Yeah." The serious expression Henry wore was replaced by his familiar grin. "Hey, did you see Stephanie's sister in there? She was looking pretty nice."

Vlad shook his head and turned the corner toward home. "Dude. Seriously. She's twelve."

3
THE HIDDEN ATTIC

VLAD ROLLED OUT OF BED and rubbed his eyes. Careful not to step on Henry, who was still snoring in his sleeping bag on the floor, he crossed the room and shut the door behind him, then stepped into the library. From the nearest recessed bookcase, he grabbed a copy of *The Theory and Practice of Telepathy* and went downstairs, where the smell of chilled blood and fried bacon greeted him. Mmm...the breakfast of champions. Aunt Nelly was at the stove and turned just as he took a seat at the long plank table. "Morning, sunshine."

Vlad blinked at her. "Morning, sulfuric acid."

"Pardon me?"

"Well, isn't it just kinda wrong to call a vampire 'sunshine'?"

"Oh. Sorry." She set a juice glass full of cool, deep red liquid in front of him, which he downed while she tapped the book. "Something interesting going on?"

Vlad ran the back of his hand across his lips, staining the

skin burgundy. "Kinda. I read someone's thoughts last night. Somebody I didn't even know."

Nelly took a seat across from him and sipped her coffee. "I thought you could only read Henry's thoughts."

"I thought so, too." He scratched his chin and flipped open the book to a page covered with yellow sticky notes.

Nelly looked pensive. "Vladimir ... you didn't ..."

Vlad scanned the page, only half listening to Nelly. When he realized what she was implying, his jaw dropped. "No! I wouldn't taste somebody's blood on purpose."

"Except for Henry's, you mean." Nelly sipped her coffee, eyeing him over her glasses.

Vlad rolled his eyes and slid the book closer to him. "Aunt Nelly, I was eight years old. Can we let that one go already?"

"Well, you said before that you were only able to read Henry's thoughts after you'd ingested some of his blood. So if you didn't taste this person's blood, how do you suppose you could read his mind?" Her tone was even, but careful.

Vlad leaned over the book and perused his various notes, theories, and scribbled thoughts on telepathy. "No idea. But then, it's not like I have an *Encyclopedia Vampirica* to consult. So far, all I have are theories."

Nelly nudged a plate of sticky buns toward him and proceeded to cover her own plate with crisp bacon, scrambled eggs, and toast. Vlad grabbed one of the sweet pastries and dropped it onto his plate while Nelly refilled his glass with the blood he would need to begin his day. Nelly had never been squeamish when it came to Vlad's diet. She was a registered nurse and went to great lengths to sneak blood from the hospital for him. Nelly chewed a bit of bacon, watching him with great interest. "So what happened at midnight?"

"No clue. We left early." Vlad shrugged. Then, thinking about his overnight guest, he asked, "Is it cool if Henry stays another night? His parents aren't going to be back until Monday afternoon."

"So long as you boys can manage to find your way to school in the morning."

As if awakened by the mere mention of his name, Henry came bounding down the stairs and burst into the kitchen with a bad case of bed head and a happy, well-rested grin. Aunt Nelly slid him an empty plate, finished her bacon, and placed a kiss on Vlad's forehead. "See you later, boys. I've got a long shift today."

Vlad ran his finger thoughtfully along the lip of his glass. "Hey, Nelly, we've got this family tree project in history. I was wondering if you could help me out."

She ruffled Henry's hair on her way to the door. "Have you checked the attic? I know your parents had some photo albums up there. They'd be more help than I would." Vlad stared after her, dumbfounded. Nelly sighed. "Honestly, Vladimir, you've lived here for three years and still don't know about the hidden attic? The door to it is a foot from your bed, for goodness' sake! I thought vampires were supposed to have ultrasensitive powers of intuition."

Vlad shrugged and picked up another sticky bun. "Don't you think if I had powers of intuition, I'd be doing better in math?"

Nelly groaned. "Let's hope you develop that next."

With the click of the front door, Vlad and Henry were left alone for the day.

They finished breakfast and settled down in front of the television, bouncing back and forth between watching cartoons and saving the world through PlayStation until morning slipped into the comfort of late afternoon. Henry had already beaten Vlad twice at *Race to Armageddon*, but on the third round, it looked as if Vlad might be making some headway. The prize, of course, was glory and riches, combined with the godlike status of having been the android to defeat the menacing alien king. But just as Vlad was raising his laser sword to strike the alien king down, Henry hit the turbo button and interrupted the blow with one of his own. Vlad dropped his controller with a groan. "I suck at this game."

"Yeah, but you can fly. I have to be better at something." Henry dropped his controller on the floor beside Vlad's and reached for his open soda can. The floor in front of the bean-bag chairs was a battlefield of open potato-chip bags and candy wrappers.

Vlad shook his head. "I can't fly. Only hover a little."

"Fly, hover, whatever . . . it's cool! Plus, if you learn how to turn invisible, just think of the terror you could be in the girls' locker room." Henry wiggled his eyebrows and took another drink. "I wonder if you'll be able to turn into animals and stuff when you get older."

At first Vlad thought Henry was kidding, but when he stole a glance at his friend, he noticed that Henry's usually jovial demeanor had turned serious. Vlad shook his head. "That's stupid."

"Think about it. In all those old stories and legends, vampires can turn into bats and wolves, and fog and stuff." Henry shrugged at Vlad and dropped his gaze to the carpeted floor between them. "It's possible."

Vlad thumbed his controller and tried not to sound too intrigued. It had been something he'd wondered about for some time. "I guess. But I'm not a hundred percent vampire anyway. My mom was human. Remember?"

Henry lowered his voice some and watched Vlad with a careful expression. "You must miss them a lot."

"All the time." Vlad held his breath for a second and tried not to give in to the sudden threat of tears that he could feel building up in his eyes. There was never a moment when he wasn't thinking about his father and the kind sparkle in his eyes, or the tender way his mother would kiss him on top of his head whenever she walked within a three-foot radius of him. Three years without them would have been impossible if it hadn't been for Nelly. It didn't matter that they weren't actually related. Nelly and his mother had been closer than sisters and that, in Vlad's mind, made Nelly family.

"It was weird how they died." Henry unplugged his controller and wrapped the cord around it.

"Yeah. People don't normally just up and burst into flames." Vlad took on a casual tone, but secretly wished Henry would forget the entire ordeal. He picked up his controller and reached for the console's reset button. "Let's play again, but this time I get to be the blue android."

"I'm hungry."

Apparently Vlad wasn't the only one with mind-reading abilities. "There's fried chicken in the fridge."

Henry disappeared into the kitchen and returned a moment later with a plate of chicken in his hands and a drumstick in his mouth. "I wuff Newwy's chippen."

Vlad wrinkled his nose, suppressing his growing nausea at the smell of cooked flesh. "Speaking of Nelly... I'd better work on that family tree. If I get another D in history, she'll kill me. When's it due, anyway?"

"Friday." Henry dropped a clean bone on the plate and looked at Vlad. "How much have you done?"

Vlad raised his eyebrows and smirked. "Does writing my name at the top of the page count?"

"I don't think so."

"Doesn't matter. I haven't done that yet anyway."

It didn't take long to find the hidden door to the attic. Vlad grabbed the flashlight from his dresser and slid in first, with

Henry following close behind him. Narrow stairs hugged the wall and curved upward, leading them to the attic room above. At the top, Vlad reached up, hoping a string to a light would be dangling down somewhere nearby. Finding one, he tugged it once and illuminated the room with a soft glow.

Henry wrinkled his nose. "Dude, what smells like cat pee?"

"You mean besides your breath?"

"Don't make me get the holy water, Vlad."

Boxes lined the walls in various towering stacks. Vlad lugged one of the boxes off a stack and placed it on the floor at Henry's feet. He reached for another, and Henry asked, "What are we looking for exactly?"

"Photo albums and birth certificates. And if we're lucky, a family tree." Vlad pulled another box down and crouched on the wood floor. He tore the packing tape away from the seam and flipped open the flaps. The top was filled with nothing of interest. Tax papers, mostly, and the occasional folder of receipts. But toward the bottom Vlad found several shoe boxes overflowing with family photos. He set them to the side and reached for another box.

By the tenth box, they'd discovered several photo albums; two small velvet boxes containing his parents' wedding bands; and a leather-bound book with a strange symbol on the front, held securely in place by thick leather straps and two brass locks. Exhausted from the search, Vlad brushed a thin coat of dust from his knees. "I guess these will have to do."

With a nod, Henry wiped a cobweb from his ear, picked up a stack of photo albums, and disappeared into the passageway.

Vlad was two steps from joining him when he spotted a cylinder poking out of a small box atop one of the stacks. He picked it up and turned it over in his hand. It was small, no more than six inches long, smooth and completely black, except for the strange gold symbol engraved at one end: three slanted lines slashed across the bottom, encased in what looked like parentheses. He slid the cylinder into his pocket before turning off the light and making his way down the stairs in the dark.

Henry was waiting for him in the bedroom, but before Vlad could show off his curious find, Aunt Nelly called up to them, "I'm home. Who wants hamburgers?" They bolted down the stairs, stomachs growling, and proceeded to help Nelly prepare their evening meal. Once the table was set and the fries had come out of the oven, she placed a bottle labeled KETCHUP on the table. When Henry reached for it, she stopped him and handed him a different bottle. "Use this one, dear. That one's for Vlad."

Vlad proceeded to squirt a healthy glob of blood onto his plate, dipped a fry in it, and bit off the end. His hamburger was raw, and the blood from it had seeped visibly into the bun. He picked it up in both hands, feeling his fangs extend at the scent of it, and tore off a bite. Henry watched in disgust as the blood dripped from Vlad's bun to his plate, but Vlad responded only by chewing. Years of watching Vlad eat had apparently not been enough to keep Henry from getting grossed out.

It was dark outside, but after their meal, the boys settled onto the porch with a drink and watched the stars peek slowly out from behind their velvet-sky blanket. On their way out the door, Nelly had handed Henry one of those juices that come in the foil bags, with the sharp-ended straw poked into one end. She'd handed Vlad a drink of blood in the same manner. They enjoyed their drinks and the lingering sounds of approaching night for several minutes before Vlad spoke. "I wonder who will sub for Mr. Craig. We can't possibly get stuck with the principal for much longer." It was one of a thousand things running through his mind. He certainly didn't want it to be Mrs. Bell, with her blue hair, crooked teeth, and equally crooked, painted-on eyebrows. For some strange reason, she always smelled like aftershave and sore-muscle cream. It really made you wonder about her after-school activities. "Mrs. Bell took over for two weeks when Mr. Craig's brother died last year."

"Can't be her. She's teaching full-time at the high school now." Henry had cupped a moth in his hands and was watching it fluttering against his palms.

Vlad took the last sip from his drink and set the container on the steps. Remembering the cylindrical object he'd found upstairs, he slipped it from his pocket and held it out for Henry's perusal. "Check this out. Found it up in the attic."

Henry released the moth, and as he slid the object out of Vlad's palm, Vlad felt a strange urge to close his hand and pull the cylinder away. Henry turned it over in his hands, admiring the engraved symbol on the bottom. "What is it?"

Vlad reached out and plucked it from Henry's hand. "No clue." He slid it back into his pocket and felt an instant blanket of comfort surround him.

Henry yawned and stretched his arms up toward the night sky. He had big, dark circles under his eyes.

Vlad yawned, too. Six in the morning came awfully early, and tomorrow he had the annoyance of some substitute teacher to deal with. With a stretch, Vlad moved up the steps and into the house, the promise of sleep heavy on his weary eyelids.

4

THE SEARCH CONTINUES

A MAN DRESSED ENTIRELY IN black looked from the crumpled newspaper photograph in his gloved hand to the boy up ahead of him who was timidly crossing the street, clutching a bag from the Stop & Shop in one hand and wearing an old thirty-five-millimeter camera around his neck. Returning his attention to the photograph, the man nodded in satisfaction and moved stealthily up the street after the boy.

The boy proceeded into a dark alleyway. The moon was full and high, casting a cool blue over the town of Bathory. Long shadows stretched across the street.

The man in black stuffed the clipping back into his pocket and quickened his pace.

The Stop & Shop bag hung limply from the boy's hand. With his other hand, the boy fiddled with the lens cap of his outdated camera, watching it far more closely than he watched where he was walking.

The man swung around him, standing in the boy's path.

It wasn't until the boy collided with the strange man that he noticed his presence. The bag fell from the boy's hand as he stumbled. "Oh jeez, sorry. I... I didn't see you there." He smiled weakly, apologetically, up at the stranger.

The man smiled, careful to keep his fangs hidden behind closed lips. "It's quite all right. Edgar Poe, isn't it?"

Eddie brushed some grime from his jeans and checked his camera for damage. "Yeah. Uh... well, Eddie, actually. Nobody but, uh... my mom calls me Edgar. Why? Do I know you?"

A large vein on Eddie's neck pulsed, sending a pang of hunger through the man's stomach. "Eddie, I was wondering if you could assist me."

The boy looked wary, but he didn't run.

The man slipped his hand into his pocket and withdrew the newspaper clipping. He held it up for the boy to see. "Do you recognize the boy standing next to you in this photo?"

Eddie glanced at the clipping. "Uh... yeah. I guess. Vlad Tod, right?"

The man licked his lips. The boy smelled like AB negative. Rare. Delectable. The champagne of blood types. "Where could I find him?"

Eddie shrugged and plucked the bag from the ground. "I... I don't know. The junior high, I guess." He stepped around the man and continued down the alleyway.

The man's stomach clenched once in hunger. He grabbed Eddie's shirt collar and opened his mouth wide, exposing his glistening fangs. "Don't you walk away from me! Tell me where he is. *Now.*"

Eddie's eyes widened with sudden terror. "What are you?"

The man lifted Eddie from the ground and pulled him closer, until his fangs were just inches from Eddie's small face. "I'm the boogeyman, Edgar. And I've come for your soul. Now tell me where I can find Vladimir Tod."

At first, the only sound coming from Eddie was the drizzle of liquid dripping from his jeans to the ground below. Then Eddie screamed.

"Edgar!" From the house at the end of the alley came a high-pitched, screeching voice that could only be Eddie's mother. "You'd better get home right now, Edgar! If I have to tell your father..."

The man released Eddie and slipped unnoticed from the alley, regretfully walking away from a warm meal and the information he needed about Tomas's son.

5
Otis Otis

VLAD ADJUSTED THE SUNGLASSES on his nose and walked up the steps to the school. He was thankful to have Henry with him. For some reason, the bullies kept their distance whenever Henry was around. Bill and Tom moved past them on the steps, but neither said a word. Principal Snelgrove was waiting at the top of the stairs, eyeing Vlad with his little mouse eyes. He twitched his nose, and Vlad chuckled out loud. The principal had hated Vlad since the first day he had been enrolled at Bathory. Bill and Tom had given him a welcoming shove down the hall, and Vlad bumped into Mrs. Kumus, who fell forward and subsequently broke her nose. It had been an accident, of course, but ever since that day, Principal Snelgrove had watched Vlad with his suspicious little rodent stare and twitched his nose distrustfully. Henry smiled as they passed the mouse man. "Good morning, Mr. Snelgrove."

Principal Snelgrove nodded, his eyes barely leaving Vlad before they'd returned again. "You'd do well to emulate your friend here, Mr. Tod." When they passed him, Vlad suppressed another chuckle. Mr. Snelgrove smelled like cheese.

At Mr. Craig's classroom door, Henry bid Vlad good-bye and wandered off down the hall. It was strange having different teachers this year, but they still sat together at lunch, goofed their way through study hall, and walked home together after school. It wasn't as much time together as either would prefer, but it would have to do. Vlad crossed the threshold of Room 6 and held his breath for a second, hoping that when he looked at the teacher's desk, he wouldn't see anyone trying to emulate crabby Mrs. Bell by glaring at him from behind her cat-eye-shaped glasses.

To Vlad's relief, the desk was unoccupied.

He walked to the back left corner of the class and, after dropping his backpack beside his desk, sat down with a weary sigh. Whoever had decided that school should start so early in the morning and last all day long needed to be hunted down and forced to watch hours of educational television without the aid of caffeine.

Meredith entered the room, brightening Vlad's day with the endearing smile on her face. She was chatting with Kara Metley, one of her two best friends. Melissa Hart was the missing link today. They were normally an inseparable trio, but Melissa had been placed in Mr. Crumble's class this year, with Henry—an arrangement that suited Henry perfectly, as he had developed a secret crush on Melissa at last year's Snow Ball, when she slapped a boy for trying to kiss her.

Henry was a strange boy.

Meredith glanced at Vlad, who shrank back in his seat and hoped she hadn't noticed he'd been watching her, and then sat at her desk. As if on cue, Kara sauntered over to his desk and dropped a note in front of him with a smile. She turned and took her place behind Meredith.

Vlad's heart took up residence in his throat. He unfolded the sheet of paper with what he considered to be casual grace and tried his best to decipher Kara's scrolling, feminine handwriting. The note's single question drove a large splinter into Vlad's self-esteem. It was short, sharp, and caused Vlad great pain.

Does Henry like Meredith?

Ouch.

And there was a tiny heart over the *i* in Meredith's name.

Double ouch.

He folded the paper back up and slipped it into the front pocket of his backpack. He'd answer it later when he had a clearer head and a lighter heart. Or ... maybe he'd just forget he ever saw it.

The door to the classroom swung open, and seconds later a tall, thin man wearing a rumpled purple top hat and a three-piece suit walked in. Under his black jacket he wore a pewter-colored vest over a crisp white shirt. Hanging from the vest's pocket was a gold pocket-watch chain. In his hand he carried an old leather doctor's bag.

After dropping his bag on the teacher's desk, he turned to the class with a bright smile. His blue eyes twinkled. "Good morning, class. I'm Mr. Otis, and I will be substituting for Mr. Craig during his absence. As my first name is the same as my last, you may call me by either, providing the obligatory title 'mister' precedes your choice."

Mr. Otis looked about the classroom, as if waiting for someone to interrupt him. When no one did, he cleared his throat and continued. "It's unfortunate that we've been brought together under these circumstances, as Mr. Craig was..." He made a clucking sound with his tongue and sat on the corner of the desk. "...is...such a fine and clearly admired teacher. But as regrettable as the situation is, I will do my best to inform and educate you in an entertaining manner."

Ever curious, Kara raised her hand. She didn't wait to be called on, but rather made her presence known with a question. "Do you know Mr. Craig?"

Mr. Otis paused for a moment, wet his lips, and said, "I'm afraid I haven't had the pleasure."

Kara wasn't quite done with her assault and, with a toss of her hair, asked, "How long have you been a teacher?"

"A long time." He turned his back to the class and began rummaging through his bag. When he turned back, his smiled had eased. He was holding what looked like a seating chart—a checkerboard of students' names. "Very long indeed. Most recently I was a full-time mythology teacher at Stokerton High, but I've taught a variety of subjects all over the world."

Out of curiosity, Vlad raised his hand, but before he could lift it more than a few inches above his desk, Mr. Otis nodded to him. Vlad dropped his hand. "So you teach English, too?"

"No. Well, that is to say, not until today." He reached into his bag again and withdrew a stack of papers. He divided the stack into fifths and dropped them on the desks in the front of the classroom. Familiar with the routine, the students took one paper and passed the rest back. "But no worries. I've already come up with a lesson plan that I'm sure you'll find both informative and entertaining."

Chelsea Whitaker didn't bother to turn around in her seat; she merely flung the last paper in the stack over her shoulder at Vlad. The paper flipped in the air and fluttered to the floor. Vlad picked it up and gave the bottom of Chelsea's seat a light kick before scanning the page, which was a list of assignments and something called "special classroom goals." There were dates typed neatly beside each assignment. Vlad wrinkled his forehead. The dates went all the way to the end of the school year. How long did this guy think he was staying?

Kara apparently had the same thought, as her hand shot into the air again. "How long will you be teaching us?"

Mr. Otis scanned the class, his eyes serious. He didn't speak.

Chelsea hissed in Kara's direction. "Don't be stupid. He'll be here until Mr. Craig comes back."

"You mean *if* he comes back." The entire class fell silent at Meredith's words. It wasn't disbelief that held their tongues, but amazement that someone had the guts to say aloud what they all feared. Meredith's cheeks flushed and she brushed a tear from the corner of her eye. Kara reached out and patted her hand after flashing Chelsea a glare.

Mr. Otis cleared his throat again, drawing everyone's attention. "Chelsea is quite right."

Of course she was. Chelsea was captain of the Cheer Squad. She was right about everything . . . or thought she was, anyway. Vlad was pretty sure Chelsea wasn't bright enough to even find her way to school each day without the assistance of her pom-pom-carrying friends and the promise of being drooled over by every thickheaded jock in the school.

Mr. Otis glanced in Vlad's general direction, plucked his watch from his vest, and flipped it open. He closed it with a snap and returned it to his pocket. "I will teach here for as long as I am needed and only as long as your teacher, Mr. Craig, remains missing. If that matter is settled, we can move on to our lesson plan." He turned to the chalkboard and drew a series of unrecognizable squiggles that were supposed to be, Vlad surmised, key points about the assignments they'd be working on. "As your teacher normally assigns you essays to test your composition skills, I will do the same. However, as I've already explained to Principal Snelgrove, I will be combining this task with my area of expertise—mythology. Each week we will study a different mythological creature, and at the end of the year, should you still be blessed with my presence, there will be a test on composition, grammar, punctuation—and mythology."

Vlad squinted at the board. One of the words looked something like *dimagom*, but that couldn't be right. The next looked a bit like *weneranlvs*. Vlad squinted harder and then looked at the paper in his hands. At the bottom was a list of mythological creatures. The first was dragons. He looked back at the board: *dimagom*. That could be dragons, he supposed. And *weneranlvs* looked suspiciously like the next word on the list: werewolves. Forgoing Mr. Otis's atrocious handwriting, Vlad read down the list.

Unicorns, griffins, centaurs, faeries, gnomes, trolls, mermaids, nymphs, banshees, zombies, witches, vampires . . .

Vlad stopped at the word *vampires* and smirked. It ought to be interesting to hear what the rest of the class thought of him. Well, most of them, anyway. There were a few whose opinions he couldn't care less about.

In front of him, Chelsea was snickering at a note Sylvia Snert had passed her. Across the top of the page was scrawled Sylvia's loopy handwriting.

This guy is a freak!!!

Chelsea whipped out her pen and scribbled something down on the note, but her shoulder blocked Vlad's view. Chelsea held the note out to Sylvia. Without a word, Mr. Otis slipped down the aisle between their desks and retrieved it. He stood in front of her and unfolded it, reading it silently with no hint of a reaction in his eyes. To Vlad's amazement, he turned and dropped the note on Sylvia's desk, returning to the front of the classroom as if nothing had happened.

"I realize that it will be a challenge for all of us to adapt to our new circumstances. Some of you may adjust more easily than others. Some of you"—he smiled at Sylvia as she read Chelsea's note—"may think I'm a freak. While others"—his eyes moved to Chelsea, who was blushing brighter than the sun—"may think I'm intriguing. Hot, some might say."

Mr. Otis raised his eyebrows. Laughter burst from the classroom, and Chelsea's face blushed even brighter. "But whatever you think of me so far, please try to keep an open mind, and if there is any way at all that I may be of assistance to you, please, don't hesitate to approach me." His eyes met Vlad's for a second and then moved across the room.

"Now, as I understand it, you are overdue for a pop quiz on punctuation."

The class let out a collective groan.

After a coma-inducing lecture on the metric system from Mr. Harold and a blissfully short video presentation in Miss Meir's biology class on "The Secret Life of Ferns," Vlad shoved his books into his already full locker, grabbed his sack lunch, and slammed the door closed.

"Somebody got up on the wrong side of the coffin." Henry was standing two lockers down, wearing an enormous grin.

Vlad snarled, suppressing a chuckle. "That may be the most obnoxious thing you've ever said to me."

"I aim to please." Henry dropped his books inside his locker. "What's going on?"

"Not much. No homework so far."

"Me neither, but I'm pretty sure ol' Batty is going to drop a quiz on us."

Vlad groaned. Batilda Motley, their eighth-grade history teacher, gave the hardest quizzes of anyone in the known universe. "That's all I need. I just had one in English class." They headed down the hall toward the lunchroom.

Henry's eyes kept darting between Vlad and every semi-attractive girl that passed them in the hall. Vlad ignored him, so Henry resorted to nudging him and pointing. "How's the new teacher, anyway?"

Vlad shrugged. "He's okay."

The lunchroom was already full by the time they got there, and as they entered, Principal Snelgrove grunted his displeasure. Vlad followed Henry through the lunch line and listened to him ramble about how busy he was going to be over winter break. His parents had finally agreed to take him and his brother on a weeklong ski trip and it seemed to be occupying most of the free space in Henry's head.

Henry looked at the food on his tray with a scowl. "I don't care what they call it. This doesn't look like pizza. It's green!"

Vlad shrugged, holding up his crumpled brown sack. "Could be worse."

Nelly always made him the same thing for lunch. He couldn't complain—not really. Vampires didn't have much of a selection when it came to ways to hide nutrients in ordinary, everyday food. Each day brought with it the same peanut-butter-and-jelly sandwich and either a couple of Twinkies or a Hostess chocolate cupcake—all discreetly filled with small capsules that Nelly had carefully injected with blood. No one ever noticed that Vlad's lunch contained any extra surprises, but a few people had offered in the past to trade him a slice of pizza or some fries for one of his Twinkies. Vlad had refused as politely as he could, reminding himself that while his lunch might be dull, it was better than his elementary school years, when he'd met his mom in the parking lot for lunch. Drinking blood out of a cooler could make you feel like such a mama's boy.

Henry led the way to their usual table near the door. When they passed Meredith, Vlad dared to smile at her.

But his smile was fleeting.

Vlad fell forward. He clutched his lunch against his chest, and when he hit the floor, he could feel the capsules inside his sandwich burst. Laughter erupted behind him, but Vlad didn't bother looking. It could be none other than Bill or Tom who'd tripped him, and if Meredith was laughing too, he didn't want to know. With Henry's assistance, he stood and grumbled at the red-stained, flattened sack. A round glob of jelly and blood clung to the front of his shirt. He picked the bag up and tossed it into the nearest garbage bin, still grumbling as he stepped into the hall.

"Where do you think you're going, Mr. Tod?" Principal

Snelgrove wrinkled his rodentlike nose, as if Vlad didn't smell very pleasant.

Vlad pulled the front of his shirt out for the principal to see. "I fell on my lunch, so I'm going to the office to call my aunt."

"There's no need for that. Charge a hot lunch today."

Vlad ran the tip of his tongue over his canine teeth and darted his eyes toward the door. "What about my shirt?"

Snelgrove snorted and clasped his hands behind his back. "There are only twenty minutes left of lunch, Mr. Tod. I suggest you hurry."

Vlad opened his mouth to speak, but stopped when he saw Snelgrove stepping closer to the door, as if Vlad might try to make a break for it. At a loss for polite words, Vlad went back to where Henry was sitting and sat across from him.

Henry wrinkled his nose at the stain on Vlad's shirt. "I can't believe he's not going to let you call Nelly."

Vlad pressed his cheek against his upturned hand and leaned on his elbow. His stomach rumbled. He laid his head on the table. It was going to be a very long afternoon.

There was a crinkling sound as half a sandwich was dropped in front of him. Vlad sighed. "You know eating that won't help." He lifted his head to a smiling Meredith, who apparently hadn't heard his grumble.

"You can have half of my sandwich, Vlad." She blushed as she glanced over at Henry, and despite the deep, calming breath he took, Vlad's heart raced. Vlad tried to speak, but that's almost impossible to do when your heart is lodged in your trachea.

Henry came to the rescue. "Thanks, Meredith."

Her smile broadened and she turned away. Her skirt swished about her knees.

Vlad felt nauseous. He smacked Henry's forearm with the back of his hand, but not as lightly as he'd intended. "What are you doing?"

"It's called being polite, dork." Henry unwrapped Meredith's sandwich and took a bite. He swallowed, looking satisfied with its taste.

Vlad scowled, wishing for a moment that he was human. "I was going to talk. I just needed a minute." Luckily, Henry didn't ask what he needed a minute to do, because Vlad really had no idea.

To Vlad's surprise, his fangs stayed safely tucked into the soft tissue of his gums all through history class and study hall. His stomach rumbled loudly as he entered Room 6, his home-room as well as his English classroom, at the end of the day. But his fangs stayed put and the bell eventually rang, releasing him from the oppression that was junior high.

Henry had waved to Vlad on his way to another student council meeting, so Vlad hung out near his locker after the bell. Vlad didn't even see Tom and Bill coming before Tom had a handful of Vlad's shirt twisted into his fist. Tom's breath smelled like peppermint, which wasn't altogether unpleasant.

Behind him, Bill was huffing up his shoulders and looking both ways down the hall for anyone who might interfere.

"What are you waiting for, goth boy?" Tom shook Vlad once before pressing him hard against the locker.

Vlad was trying his best not to open his mouth—not for fear of what he might say, but because he could feel a gnawing urge to bite Tom out of spite. He ran his tongue over his teeth and found his fangs poking out, reacting to the subtle scent of blood rushing beneath Tom's skin. "I'm not goth."

Tom pulled him away from the locker and slammed him up against it again, sending a loud clang into the hall. "What?"

Vlad straightened his shoulders. "I said I'm not goth."

Tom looked back at Bill, who rolled his eyes. When Tom turned back to Vlad, his eyes were rolling, too. "You goth sack of crap. Don't even know you're goth!"

Not that Vlad had anything against being goth, really. He'd seen the goth kids hanging around the steps of Bathory High at night, cloaked in black and looking for a way out of small-town life. They weren't so different from him, with their black hair, black clothes, and dark humor. In fact, Vlad had secretly wished he would be lucky enough someday to find friends that seemed so like him. Henry was great, but sometimes it was really hard being his shadow.

Tom shook him again, apparently not satisfied that Vlad wasn't quivering with fear. But Vlad, despite preferring almost everything else to spending a moment with Tom. wasn't feeling very afraid. In fact. he wasn't feeling afraid at all. He was feeling ... hungry.

Holding his breath. Vlad pushed with his mind. Then, with a strange. dizzying rush of blood to his head, he began to feel completely irritated.

What was this kid's problem. anyway? Why wasn't he crying and begging to be let go? And what was he staring at? Tom glanced over his shoulder at Bill, who merely shrugged. He pulled back his fist. One quick punch would do it. and then he could slip down the hall to his mom's waiting car. Mom would be a real pain if he was late for ballet. He hated dance. All those froufrou boys and the stupid leotard. But she kept making him go—three years apparently hadn't been enough. At least Bill didn't know. Bill thought he was going to his uncle's every Friday to learn how to make pipe bombs. If he knew the truth ...

Vlad smirked and felt his mind pull out of Tom's thoughts. It had been easy. Maybe it was the hunger that made it easy. Without a glance at Tom's fist. he whispered. "You'd better hurry. ballerina boy. You wouldn't want to be late."

Tom blinked. He lowered his fist and looked back at Bill, who was punching his palm and eyeing Vlad. Vlad's smirk spread into a smile. "What would Bill say if he knew you were dancing around in tights with other guys? Think he'd be open-minded? Understanding?" Vlad followed Tom's gaze to Bill, who'd stopped practicing on his fist and was looking at Tom expectantly.

Vlad pressed his lips together, despite the gnawing urge to flash his fangs.

Tom relaxed his grip on Vlad's shirt and stepped back. He grabbed Bill's sleeve and they moved down the hall, away from Vlad. Bill was whispering questions, but Tom silenced him with a shove.

In the window across from where he stood, Vlad caught his reflection. He looked paler, older, and positively fierce. He smiled, revealing his perfect white fangs.

It had turned out to be a good day after all.

6

SECRETS AND SANCTUARY

"D RESSED AS I AM, what do I look like to you?" Mr. Otis looked about the classroom. Several students fiddled with objects on their desks in response. Some met his gaze with glazed eyes of indifference. "Come on, first thing that pops into your head."

A small voice broke the silence. "A homeless guy?"

Stephanie Brawn shot her hand up. Her tone was matter-of-fact. "A mortician."

"A zombie?" Carl squeaked. Carl was one of the quieter students. Lanky, shy. It always surprised Vlad to hear his voice.

Mr. Otis pointed a long finger at Carl. His eyes twinkled. "Yes. As you seemed to enjoy my unicorn costume last week and my troll costume the week before, I thought I'd choose something a bit less obvious this time. I wore this as inspiration for the project we'll be undertaking this week."

Mr. Otis turned to his bag, where he retrieved a hefty stack of papers and began passing them to each student. Once the papers were handed out, he returned to his perch on the corner of the desk, a proud smile on his face. He searched their eyes, obviously expecting wonderment and curiosity, but his smile slipped when he found only disappointment. Even Vlad, who'd come to enjoy having Mr. Otis as a teacher over the past few weeks and found the study of such things fascinating, slumped down in his seat. New projects always started out sounding cool, but before you knew it, the teacher had glitter and construction paper strewn about the room and you were getting fitted for some stupid costume. Vlad decided that teachers' ideas were a lot like bunches of garlic—intriguing from afar, but up close sadly sickening and, if you weren't careful, deadly. Still, he felt sorry for Mr. Otis, who, like so many substitutes, was trying to make an impression.

Vlad raised his hand and asked, "Will this be an oral report or written?"

"I'm glad you asked." Mr. Otis glanced down at the papers on his desk and back at the class. "Since I first began teaching you, we've been learning the folklore and history of a different mythological creature every week. This week we will embark on the study of supernatural beings, and at the end of our studies, you will each be turning in a thousand-word essay on one of those supernatural creatures, as well as giving an oral presentation near the end of February."

Mr. Otis turned to the blackboard with a spring in his step and scribbled down a list of slightly crooked words. He turned back to the class and nodded at the intrigued looks he saw on their faces. Reaching into his bag, he retrieved a handful of small, folded papers. Mr. Otis stuffed them into his hat and said, "These will be no ordinary reports. I want you to write them as if you were the creature you draw from my hat. Tell me how you feel, what your strengths are, your weaknesses, any special abilities you may have. Tap into what makes you a witch, a werewolf, a vampire, and so on. Show me the true nature of yourself."

Vlad sank farther into his seat. Hiding his true nature was a daily chore and certainly not something he wanted to expose in front of the class. People would panic. Meredith would cringe. And he could only imagine how closely Principal Snelgrove would watch him after learning his secret. As Mr. Otis began his slow trip around the room, stopping at each desk and holding out the hat, Vlad crossed his fingers under the desk and hoped that the mathematical odds would be with him and he'd draw *zombie* or *warlock*—anything *but* his true nature.

In front of him, Chelsea Whitaker was pouting over her pick. She lifted her furrowed brow to Mr. Otis, who merely smiled and held the hat out to Vlad. Vlad reached in and pulled out a slip of paper.

Vlad cupped it in his hand, willing it to read anything but *vampire*. He took a deep breath, held it until his lungs burned, and opened his hand.

The paper was blank. Vlad blinked, and when he looked up at Mr. Otis, he noticed that his teacher was watching the slip of paper with decided interest. Feeling more than a little curious and only slightly stupid, Vlad flipped the paper over and read his assigned creature.

Werewolf.

A sigh escaped Vlad before he realized it was he who'd made it. At the moment, he couldn't think of a more pleasant word to read, and so he read it once again. *Werewolf.*

He could do werewolf. Howling at the moon, fear of all things silver, inexplicable urge to sniff the butts of people he met on the street. Oh yeah, piece of cake.

Mr. Otis's hand clenched into a tight fist. Then, just as Vlad's muscles relaxed, the letters scrawled on the small rectangle of paper blurred. At first Vlad thought his eyes were simply losing focus, so he squeezed them closed, but when he opened them again, the letters were rearranging themselves, moving about the piece of paper like tiny figure skaters. Some of the lines blended with others, forming new letters.

Vlad's jaw dropped, and as if on command, the letters stopped moving. Vlad read the new word they'd formed aloud. "Vampire?"

He couldn't do vampire! Fear of the sun, craving for blood, inability to enjoy Italian food, everything that he really was? This was going to suck.

Mr. Otis relaxed his fist and leaned in toward Vlad. His smile, kind and warm at the front of the class, seemed sly and twisted up close. "A wise choice, Vladimir. I'll be looking forward to reading your perception of vampires."

As if they shared a secret, Mr. Otis tapped his forefinger against his temple and pointed to Vlad, who looked quickly back at the paper he'd chosen and read the word once again: *vampire*. There it was, in plain English. Could he have misread it? No way. It just wasn't possible. *Werewolf* and *vampire* weren't similar at all. He could understand the mistake if the paper had said something like *vumpine*, but *werewolf* looked nothing like *vampire*.

And what about the moving letters? Had he imagined it? Aunt Nelly would say he'd been under a lot of stress lately, that it had been a trick of the mind, that handwriting couldn't move around on its own. She'd probably be right, but the entire event, imagined or real, still freaked Vlad out.

"Now, back to zombies," Mr. Otis began as he returned to the front of the class. "Any guesses on what their diet consists of?"

Morning passed quickly into afternoon and Vlad entered the lunchroom, finding Henry sitting at the table near the window, waving him over. Henry shoved an entire Hostess cupcake into his mouth and grinned. The white filling squished out between Henry's teeth, eliciting a chuckle from Vlad.

Vlad sat across from Henry and slid the sandwich out from his brown paper sack. He bit into the bread and one of the capsules of blood burst open, spraying the roof of his mouth with crimson sweetness. He swallowed the liquid and finished his meal. After tossing the empty bag and stained, soggy plastic wrap into the garbage, he let out a loud burp. "Excuse me."

Henry laughed and offered him a cupcake, which Vlad immediately stuffed into his mouth. Sure, human food didn't help him out nutritionally, but some of it just tasted good.

Henry asked, "So when are you asking Meredith to the Snow Ball? It's coming up soon, you know."

Principal Snelgrove passed behind Henry and slowed his steps, peering over Henry's shoulder at Vlad.

Vlad shrugged. "I'm not sure I'm going to."

Henry said, "Why not? You've only been crushing on her since the third grade. And a girl like Meredith you have to ask well in advance."

Behind Henry, Vlad could see Meredith talking with her girlfriends. When she looked over at Henry, her blush deepened. Vlad shrugged again. "Better to be crushing *on* her than have my heart crushed *by* her. Besides, I think she likes someone else."

Henry slanted his eyes. "Like who? You're making excuses again. Just ask her, Vlad. She's just a girl. Worst thing she can do is say no."

But that wasn't the worst thing Meredith could do. She could laugh. She could tell her friends all about how the pathetic, pale kid asked her on a date, and word could reach Bill and Tom—more fuel for the fire. Vlad would rather die.

Or worse, go to the dance alone.

Mr. Otis, who'd also taken on Mr. Craig's homeroom duties, was leaning back in his chair, his feet propped carelessly up on the desktop, when Vlad approached him after the final bell. The teacher wasn't wearing a smile, but more the hint of one. "The infamous Vladimir Tod. What can I do for you?"

Vlad couldn't recall ever having done anything remotely infamous, but he nodded and withdrew the scrap of paper from his shirt pocket. "I'd really rather pick again, if you don't mind."

Mr. Otis sat up and clucked his tongue. "That wouldn't be fair to the rest of the class."

Vlad didn't much care what was fair, only that he was a little more than hesitant to reveal the details of his true identity. He had hoped only to discuss vampire lore with the class, having become quite adept at separating the truth from the enormous number of lies spread by various media over the years. He'd much rather write an essay on werewolves or warlocks anyway, even though a thousand words on any of the creatures on the list didn't strike him as terribly exciting. Vlad lifted his shoulders and dropped them again slowly. He had no reason to offer but the truth. "I'd just really rather pick again."

Mr. Otis paused with his hand on the brim of the top hat. Then, with an assenting nod, he nudged the hat toward Vlad, who reached in and withdrew another slip of paper.

Vlad gazed at the paper with direct intensity, wondering if the letters would move this time. He unfolded it and furrowed his brow.

Vampire.

Mr. Otis stood and, after emptying the remaining slips of paper into his bag, popped his hat onto his head. "Fate can be cruel, Mr. Tod. I look forward to your oral presentation from a vampire's point of view."

Vlad's feet felt like they were frozen to the ground. There was no getting out of this, as far as he could tell. And why did Mr. Otis seem so insistent, so anxious that Vlad tackle the very topic he wanted most to avoid?

The answer was easy.

Because teachers, no matter how kind, no matter how friendly, are sadistic and evil to the core.

Vlad swung his backpack over his shoulder and slipped out the door without so much as a grunt or a glance in Mr. Otis's direction. Vlad thought about Mr. Craig and wished that wherever his teacher was, he was safe. And would return soon.

"It can't be all that bad. Maybe you just need to shift your outlook a bit." Nelly smiled.

Vlad found little comfort in her words. "You don't understand. That paper said *werewolf,* not *vampire,* when I pulled it out of the hat. I know it did."

Nelly pursed her lips. After a moment of silence, she said,

"I think you've just been under a lot of stress. Words don't re-write themselves, Vladimir. It's just not possible."

Vlad wrinkled his forehead and picked at the corner of his English book. "And who wears a top hat? This guy is weird."

Nelly sighed. "Vladimir, give him a chance. You don't even know him."

But Vlad wasn't sure he wanted to know Mr. Otis. "I don't know, Nelly. Something just doesn't feel right."

Nelly flashed him one of her overly concerned looks. Vlad didn't want to argue and he certainly didn't want Nelly think-ing he was crazy. He offered a smile, plastic as it was, and flipped open his notebook. "You're probably right."

"This project isn't all bad, Vladimir dear. You can finally get all your secrets off your chest without worrying about be-ing exposed. And who knows? It might be fun to speculate about future abilities. And you could throw in some of those silly stereotypes just for laughs." She sipped the last of her tea and yawned. "I need to get some rest. Don't stay up too late."

"I won't. But *Nosferatu* is on cable tonight, so I'll probably stay up to watch it." He wasn't sure why exactly, but the older, the cheesier a vampire movie was, the more it lifted his spir-its. *Nosferatu* was his favorite, as the pointy-eared, bald-headed monster had sent him into hysterical fits of laughter on a number of occasions. Nelly found the movies ignorant and in-sulting, but supported Vlad's fondness for them just the same.

"Finish your homework first." Nelly was already across the

room when she paused and threw him another worried glance. "You don't sleep enough."

"Aunt Nelly."

"Okay, okay. I'll see you in the morning." She slipped upstairs and out of sight.

Vlad took out the instruction sheet Mr. Otis had handed out, and scanned it. Maybe he should get started on the essay right away so that it wasn't looming over him for the rest of the term. Determined to get it over with, he opened his notebook, picked up a pen, and began to write.

My name is Vladimir Tod, and I am a vampire.

He sat back for a moment, examining what he'd written. It had been easier than he'd expected to confess his true nature, so Vlad tightened his grip on the pen and continued to write. He went into the details of his hovering ability and telepathy, exploring the question of why he had them. With a laugh, he then threw in speculation on why vampires had no reflection and couldn't be photographed. It was a ridiculous notion, as Vlad had never had problems with either. He'd managed to show up in every school photo since kindergarten and, to date, he hadn't heard anyone on the yearbook committee complain. And judging by the slew of pictures he had of his dad, it wasn't much of a problem for other vampires, either.

After a paragraph on how stupid people were to think that any living being could live forever, he paused again and wrote one final line.

I'm not a monster. I'm just me.

A thousand words had come much easier than Vlad had expected.

He read the paper over again and resisted the urge to erase nearly every word.

After scarfing several handfuls of potato chips and drinking a blood bag, Vlad flopped down on the couch and immersed himself in the world of Count Orlok—the creature known in the cinematic world simply as Nosferatu. The movie had just reached the part where Count Orlok is traveling by raft when Vlad's mind began to wander down whatever road had taken Mr. Craig from Bathory Junior High.

Rumors at school had echoed the suspicions of both the police and the media. Someone was responsible for the disappearance of the well-liked eighth-grade teacher, and no one knew whom to blame. People were saying that nothing seemed to be amiss. Mr. Craig's car still sat in his driveway. His belongings remained in their usual arrangement. His bank account hadn't been touched. If Mr. Craig had vanished of his own accord, he'd left with nothing but the clothes he wore, and that wouldn't have gotten him very far from the small suburban town of Bathory.

Forgoing the rest of the film, Vlad clicked off the television and tiptoed upstairs.

Amenti—Nelly's fluffy, plump black cat—rubbed against Vlad's legs. Vlad stroked her soft fur, and she arched her back in response. Nelly had named Amenti after the Egyptian goddess who was said to have guarded the gateway to the after-life. The goddess, much like the cat, had beautiful hair and practically lived in trees. It was a fitting name, as Vlad had come home on a number of occasions to find Amenti's pudgy body wedged in the lowest crook of the old oak tree in the backyard, though he was confounded to explain just how she had managed to waddle her way up there.

After a brief interval in his bedroom to retrieve his jacket and one of the many photo albums he'd found in the attic, Vlad grabbed several candles from the drawer in the library and stuffed them into his coat pocket. Amenti nudged his ankle with her forehead, demanding his attention once again. Vlad reached down and scratched behind her ears. She purred happily and slinked away. He moved down the stairs, careful not to make a sound, and slipped out the front door into the brisk night.

The streets were empty and dark. Vlad avoided the sidewalks, choosing instead the small beaten paths that wove between this house and that—the mark of many kids before him who'd been in search of the quickest route between school and home. Vlad rounded each corner with a careful step and threw a glance in each direction. He hadn't yet been caught out after curfew, but there was always a chance that he might be.

He reached the side of Bathory High and paused briefly when he heard laughter. It was likely just the goth kids who often occupied the high school's steps after dark. Vlad slipped around to the back of the school. Bathory High School had been built up in the hollowed-out remains of a very large, very old Catholic church. It was well known that the church had been deserted sometime in the mid-1800s, as a result of some sort of horrific affair, but locals had protested tearing the historical building down. Then, nearly a hundred years later, a wealthy businessman had purchased the property and developed it into what had been known as Bathory Preparatory Academy. Twenty years later, the school became a public institution.

It was probably the most interesting thing about Bathory.

When Vlad reached the back of the school, he looked around to be certain he was alone, then closed his eyes and willed his body upward. His feet left the ground and he floated up to the school's belfry.

The bell tower was large and square. Several arching windows lined its walls, open to the elements at all times. Vlad walked along the ledge and looked down on the group of teenagers on the front steps. They wore black from head to toe, merely shadows amid more shadows. Vlad smiled. He slipped inside one of the windows and dug the candles from his pockets. Small mounds of wax dotted the room—remnants from previous visits. Vlad placed the new candles on the floor and lit their wicks with a lighter he kept on one of the windowsills, illuminating the room with a soft glow.

The bells had long been removed from the tower, and the only door had been sealed shut when the building became a school. The only way in or out was through the windows, and the ground was four stories below them. The room was large and empty but for several books that had been banned from both the school and the town's library and a framed photograph that had been propped against a stack of stray red bricks at the center of the room.

Vlad knelt and moved the candle closer to the picture. "Hi, Dad."

Tomas Tod smiled back—a portrait of happiness forever fixed.

Vlad looked around his sacred space and sighed. "I should get a chair."

He placed the photo album on the floor near the candle. The cover was green leather. On the front was a family crest. Vlad flipped to the first page and smiled at the photograph of his mother, Mellina. She was standing near an old car, looking young and pretty. Her eyes twinkled. On the hood of the car sat a younger version of Nelly, wearing a bright, happy grin. Vlad turned the page.

He saw pictures of his parents' wedding, of their popular Halloween parties, of their lips locked in happy, wedded bliss. He ran his hand across one photograph of Tomas crouching in front of Mellina's swollen, pregnant belly. His hands cupped her tummy. Vlad's smile faltered some and he closed the album.

This was all he had left of his family. Pictures and memories.

He lay back on the dusty floor. Moonlight shone through the windows, painting the darkest areas of the room in pale blue. The candle's flame flickered and, just as the first tear squeezed from Vlad's eye, the light went out. Vlad lay in the darkness and released his pain the only way he knew how. He cried.

At some point, he must have fallen asleep.

Vlad rubbed his eyes. He stood and slipped out onto the ledge, leaving the photo album behind with the rest of his treasures. The town was still very dark. Vlad looked down, hoping to catch another glimpse of his fellow nightwalkers, but the goth teens had gone.

He was alone.

As he floated down to the ground, Vlad looked back up at the belfry. It was the highest point of Bathory, and each time Vlad went there, he was the closest he'd ever been to leaving the small town behind. He darted between the houses and paused once his front door was in sight.

Mr. Craig's house was only two streets over, directly behind Henry's. He slipped between the houses and smiled at the sight of Mr. Craig's tiny bungalow. The porch glowed dimly from the streetlight on the corner, a welcoming hue of white on the stark black of night. He stepped onto the porch and rang the bell. As childish as he knew it was, he was half hoping, half expecting Mr. Craig to open the door and lecture him on why it was rude to visit someone's home in the middle of the night. But no one answered.

The screen door screeched as he pulled it open. He knocked loudly on the inner door, then stopped as it opened inward. Vlad looked over his shoulder at the quiet street. He stepped inside and closed the door behind him. The police had been here a zillion times, so Henry had said, but they might have missed something—they had to have missed something—or Mr. Craig would have been found by now. And why was the door left unlocked? Bathory cops were bumbling idiots, sure, but didn't they know how to lock up a possible crime scene?

Beside the door sat a dark mahogany hat tree, adorned with Mr. Craig's jacket and scarf. An umbrella was looped over one of the pegs. Vlad moved through the hall with slow, sure steps. The house smelled like dust, as if no one had been here to fill the air with the scent of pine cleaners and bleach in a long time. He half expected to see cobwebs. But he was sure the scent was a trick of his wild imagination.

Vlad's shoes moved soundlessly over the bare wood floors as he approached the kitchen at the end of the hall. A closet door stood open, blocking his path, so he closed it. A painting hung on the wall opposite him of a red-haired woman holding a sword in front of her chest. Her eyes were closed as if she were sleeping, which made no sense, what with the raging fires painted around her. He wondered if it was a painting of Joan of Arc, the famous French heroine Mr. Craig had told him about at the beginning of the school year.

Up ahead, something moved.

Vlad didn't know what, or who, it was, but something had crossed the open door at the end of the hall. It may have been black, but he couldn't be sure, as there was only a little light illuminating his view.

Swallowing his fear, Vlad took a step toward the door, where the ... thing ... had been. "Hello?"

A rustling sound answered him, followed by gunshots. *Bang! Bang!* Vlad ducked, covering his head with his arms, as if flesh alone could protect against bullets. *Bang! Bang!* Risking a shot to the head, Vlad lowered his arms and tried to get a clear view of his assailant. No one stood at the end of the hall, and a glance over his shoulder showed the similar lack of anyone by the front door, armed or otherwise. *Bang! Bang!*

Vlad rolled his eyes and stood. He moved into the kitchen and pulled the back screen door closed. The banging ceased.

Some hero he was.

After an extensive search of the living room, dining room, and kitchen, Vlad decided to continue his search upstairs. So far, nothing seemed amiss at all. But Vlad couldn't bring himself to believe Mr. Craig would just vanish without a word to him. They'd been more than student and teacher—they were friends. He turned on his heel and walked back down the hall to the stairs near the front door. In the darkness, the coat tree looked a bit like a skeleton.

Vlad froze.

On one of the pegs hung a rumpled, purple silk top hat.

Vlad slipped the hat off its peg and looked inside. Embroidered in shiny black thread were the initials *O.O.*—Otis Otis. His forehead creased in wonder and disbelief. Why had Mr. Otis lied about knowing Mr. Craig? Vlad looked around, suddenly wondering if he was alone in the house. He was almost positive the hat hadn't been hanging there when he'd entered.

With a glance at the stairs, Vlad quietly returned the hat to its peg. Was Mr. Otis in the house right now? Nelly was right. Vlad didn't know the guy, but could he trust him? What business did he have running around Mr. Craig's house in the middle of the night? Vlad looked at the stairs again. He should march right up and demand to know what Mr. Otis was doing here.

Vlad took a step toward the stairs and paused. What if Mr. Otis had something to do with Mr. Craig's disappearance? What if he was returning to the scene of the crime?

The noble thing would be to leave the house and head straight for the police station to tell them everything he knew.

But what did he know?

Only that what looked suspiciously like Mr. Otis's hat had been hanging on Mr. Craig's hat tree when Vlad had gone into the house to look around. Vlad doubted very much it would be enough to convince that idiot Officer Thompson of anything. Plus, Vlad might get in serious trouble for breaking curfew . . . not to mention breaking and entering.

He'd do better to spend a few more weeks watching his new teacher and seeing if the odd feeling in his stomach would go away.

Vlad stepped outside, pulling the door closed behind him. His toe caught the edge of the welcome mat, sending him stumbling. With a grumble, he kicked the mat. But before it slid back into place, he spotted a strange symbol carved into the wood of the porch. With a gaping mouth, he pulled the mat back again.

Three slanted lines slashed across the porch—all encased in what looked like parentheses.

7
FEEDING TIME

KATE DONAHUE BRUSHED STRANDS of hair out of her eyes, sweeping them back from her sweaty face as her feet met the pavement in rhythmic, slapping steps. Glancing at her watch as she made her third round of the track that outlined Bathory Park, she grunted. Robert would be irate that she'd gone for a run after dark.

She rounded a park bench and, brushing her hair out of her face once more, slowed her steps to cool down. She pressed her fingers to her neck and counted her pulse beats silently.

One...two...three...

Except for Kate, the park was empty. Large pools of light from the streetlamps spotted the lush grounds. Kate breathed in through her nose and out through her mouth; her breath was released into the air in the form of wispy clouds.

Eight...nine...ten...

She wiped the sweat from her eyes with the back of her hand. When she pulled her hand away, she saw a man, dressed in black, standing by the nearest streetlight. Kate felt her heart jump and mentally slapped herself. Robert's panicky concerns were making her edgy.

Thirteen... fourteen... fifteen...

She slowed her steps even more and then began to stretch her calves. Her muscles were on fire with a pleasant burn. She took a healthy swallow from her water bottle and glanced in the direction of the man, who hadn't changed his posture or expression, but now seemed to be standing ten feet closer.

Kate took another drink and slipped her bottle back into her duffel bag. She picked the bag up and, with another glance at the man in black, turned toward the parking lot. Maybe Robert was right. Maybe even a little slice of nowhere like Bathory wasn't safe all the time. She passed under another pool of light and her water bottle tumbled out of her bag. It smacked the paved path and popped open. With a groan, Kate bent down and stuffed it back into the bag with a grumble.

"Excuse me, madam."

With a curse under her breath, Kate looked up at the man and smiled as pleasantly as she could manage. "Yes?"

A flash of skin—pale, smooth, flawless skin—passed before her eyes, and the man had her by the throat. He dragged her away from the light, toward the nearby grove of trees. Kate kicked and tried to scream, but couldn't find the breath to call for help. She dug her heels into the grass, to no avail. He pulled her along as if she weighed no more than a heavy back-pack and slammed her against the trunk of a large maple tree. His fingers were still pressing into her neck, but he relaxed them enough for her to breathe.

Kate's lungs burned as she gasped for air. "What do you want? I'll do anything! Just please don't hurt me!" Her words were mangled whispers, as if her voice box had been dam-aged beyond the ability to voice the terror she was feeling.

The man opened his mouth wide, exposing a pair of long, white, slick fangs. Kate screamed her whispers of protest.

He pinned her against the tree, and though she wriggled, he sank his teeth easily into her smooth neck and drank.

Her heartbeat slowed in her ears. She could feel herself sliding down the tree trunk as the strength left her body. Tears coated her cheeks. "Why are you doing this?"

The man pulled away with a low chuckle. "Because I enjoy it. Besides, like any living creature, I must feed."

Kate fell to the ground and lifted the great weight of her head so that she was looking up at her attacker. She couldn't run. She could barely speak, but she had to buy time until help arrived. "Please don't kill me," she sobbed. "I'll give you anything."

The man in black paused and glanced over his shoulder, as if checking for passers-by. "There is nothing you have that I want, except your blood." He crouched then and tilted her head to the side, examining her wounds with childlike fascination before bending closer to resume his meal.

"I can give you money. Take my car. Anything, please."

"Unless you can provide me with the Tod boy, you have nothing for me."

"Vladimir Tod?" Kate spoke quickly in strangled whispers, though her throat burned and ached.

The man paused.

"I know his aunt. I see her every Tuesday at the Stop & Shop."

The man relaxed his grip on her and sat back on his haunches. "And the boy? Where does he live?"

"With her, as far as I know." Kate swallowed. She could taste her own blood. She managed to croak out, "Will you let me go?"

"No. I'm still hungry." After a pause the span of a heartbeat, the man latched his mouth firmly to her open wound. He drank until the sky above became a blur of blackish blue, and as he walked away, Kate watched his shoes move two steps through the fallen leaves before she passed into the oblivion of death.

8
THE BOOK

M R. OTIS STOOD BEFORE the class, a black, pointy hat resting comfortably atop his head. "Everybody knows about witches, right? I'm sure you've read about them in one fairy tale or another. *Hansel and Gretel, Snow White, The Wizard of Oz*—they all had witches. Green-faced, warts on their noses, black cats hanging around all the time. Generally not very nice old ladies. Not exactly the grandma's house you want to go to for milk and cookies.

"In recent years, witches have come into a much better light than those with poisoned apples, or an obsession with gaudy footwear, due to a popular book series set at a magic school. Much of our discussion will be…" Mr. Otis paused with his arm raised before the blackboard, clutching a bit of chalk. His pose matched that of Meredith, who was raising her arm with a question. "Yes, Meredith?"

Meredith was looking extremely feminine today, Vlad

noted with a wistful sigh. Her hair was swept up into the slight curl of a ponytail, which was tied with a blush-pink ribbon that matched her dress. She lowered her hand and parted her lips, shimmering with berry-pink lip balm, to speak. "I'm sorry, Mr. Otis, but you're wrong about witches."

Mr. Otis returned the chalk to the long aluminum tray that ran beneath the blackboard. He seemed more intrigued than annoyed at her interruption, and when he smiled at her, Vlad could tell his interest was genuine. "Am I?"

Meredith brushed a stray brunette curl from her cheek. "My friend Catherine and her family practice witchcraft. There's really nothing mythological about it." To emphasize her point, Meredith removed her berry lip balm from her desk and glossed her lips.

Mr. Otis looked from Meredith to the chalkboard. He pinched his chin between his thumb and the knuckle of his pointer finger and looked the class over a moment before speaking. "Indeed. You are absolutely correct." His lips curled in a smile. "However, there is a stark difference between the reality of witchcraft and what the Grimm Brothers would have you believe. It is the mythical variety that we will be focusing our attention on today." He returned to the board and paused. "In truth, I believe that all of the creatures we are studying have existed or do exist, in some form or another."

Sylvia Snert didn't bother raising her hand, nor did she even attempt to hide her doubt. "You think werewolves are real?"

"As a matter of fact, Miss Snert, I know that they are. Lycanthropy is the psychological belief that one is, in fact, a werewolf. It is well documented and still prevalent even today. And an entire family in Mexico has been reported to suffer from a rare genetic mutation that causes furlike hair to grow all over their bodies. It is known as the 'Werewolf Disorder.'"

Sylvia snorted. "And vampires? Are they real, too?"

Mr. Otis closed his eyes for a moment and then opened them again; irritation mixed with his tone. "Of course. Take our own Mr. Tod, for example."

Vlad couldn't breathe. Every eye in the class was on him. He shrank down in his seat, trying to be invisible. If he succeeded, he'd have to remember to take a trip to the girls' locker room, just for Henry's sake.

"He bears the first name of the most famous vampire of all, Vlad Tepes—also known as Vlad the Impaler. A Romanian prince who was known to take his supper among his tortured enemies and drink their blood with his meal as if it were a fine wine. He was a vicious, cruel, ingenious man." Mr. Otis flipped open a book on his desk and regarded Sylvia with a stern glance. "But Vlad's day will come. Today we are talking about witches."

Vlad relaxed and straightened in his seat. He smiled when Sylvia shot him a glare. It was pretty cool to know you shared a name with somebody famous—even if they were famous for human slaughter.

The rest of the day flew by, with Vlad daydreaming during most of it. When the final bell rang, Vlad slipped his books quickly into his backpack and, hoisting it over his shoulder, rushed toward the door. If he hurried, he might make it to the corner before Bill and Tom noticed his exit. Despite his mind-reading episode with Tom several weeks ago, their antics had continued, if not worsened. Vlad had had his books knocked out of his hands and his backpack run up the flagpole more times than he could count. He didn't care to repeat the experiences.

Mr. Otis was still at his desk, pen in hand, that now-familiar scrawl scribbled out on several papers in front of him. "Could I have a word with you, Vlad?"

Vlad hesitated, wondering if Mr. Otis had seen him in Mr. Craig's house the other night. He hadn't noticed anything particularly suspicious since then, but he'd been watching. Vlad dropped his bag on the floor, contemplating whether Bill and Tom would wait for him after school. They'd done it before and would again, he wagered, but there was no way he could rush off when his teacher had told him to stay. "Am I in trouble?"

Mr. Otis raised his eyebrows in surprise. "No, no. Nothing like that. I merely wished to speak with you about a personal matter."

"Oh yeah?" Vlad had no clue what sort of personal matter his teacher might want to discuss with him.

Then it hit him.

Maybe Mr. Otis wanted to reveal that he had known Mr. Craig, that he knew something about Mr. Craig's disappearance, or worse, that he'd been involved. Vlad's imagination seized every resource in his brain and flashed chilling images of abduction and murder through his mind. Some of the scenes were quite grisly and made his stomach twist and turn. He squeezed his eyes shut and opened them again, his imagination's wanderings once more under control.

Mr. Otis shifted in his seat, as if the subject of personal matters was making him uncomfortable. "I met your aunt yesterday at the market. She inquired about my perhaps joining you both for dinner some evening, but I told her I'd like to discuss it with you first. Does that make you uncomfortable at all?"

Of course it made him uncomfortable. And a little nauseous, too, considering that his aunt had asked his teacher on what could be considered a date. But it would be the perfect opportunity to get Mr. Otis to spill his guts on just why his top hat was hanging in Mr. Craig's house. Vlad picked up his bag again and swung it over his shoulder. "I don't mind, but I should warn you ... she's a terrible cook." Vlad smiled and so did Mr. Otis. "I better go, though. Henry's waiting." He turned and slipped out the door, hoping that Henry was indeed waiting for him or, at the very least, that Bill and Tom weren't.

▼　▼　▼

Vlad rolled over and cursed at the alarm clock on his night-stand. It was almost two in the morning, and he still couldn't sleep.

He picked up the large book he'd found weeks ago in the attic and moved toward the door. The book was several inches thick; the leather of its cover felt old and warm in his hands. Two big buckles were strapped across the front. Vlad ran his fingers over the locks thoughtfully and wondered, not for the first time, what the pages contained. A rebel floorboard near the door betrayed him and squeaked loudly under his foot. He placed his ear against the door and listened. Nothing. The door creaked as he pulled it open and peered into the dark library. It was empty, but for the sleeping presence of Amenti.

Amenti was curled up in the leather wingback chair in the corner. She raised her head, blinked, and meowed at Vlad, her tone that of a question. "It's just me, Amenti." He slid open the candle drawer as quietly as he could.

"What are you doing up?"

Nelly's voice startled him and he fumbled, nearly dropping the mysterious tome on his foot. Steadying his hands, Vlad smiled sheepishly at her. "Couldn't sleep. What about you?"

She offered a chastising head shake, and then her smile bloomed. "Me neither. Want some tea?"

By tea she meant, of course, microwaved blood in a teacup, but Nelly had such a sweet way of making him feel completely normal. Not that being a vampire was bizarre or anything, certainly not abnormal. But sometimes, when he was putting on his sunblock in the morning or when Henry would describe the incredible lasagna his mom made, he felt a small pang of jealousy for humans. They had it so easy. Try worrying about your fangs popping out at inopportune moments or having to avoid garlic because one taste could make you deathly ill or forcing yourself to stay awake all day even though down to the cellular level, you were more of a night person. Oh yeah—humans had it way easy, as far as Vlad was concerned.

He followed Nelly down to the kitchen, where she dropped the kettle on the stove and heated up a cup of tangy blood for Vlad in the microwave. Vlad dipped a chocolate-chip cookie into his cup and bit into it. Something about the taste of chocolate and blood mixed together in his mouth just felt right. Vlad sipped from his cup and picked up another cookie.

Nelly dunked a tea bag into the steamy water in her mug. She ran a curious finger over the symbol on the front of the book. "What are you reading? I don't remember this. Is it one of mine?"

"I found it in the attic. I'm not reading it, though." He pointed to the locks with his cookie, still tinged deep red with his "tea." "It's locked and I have no idea how to open it."

Nelly tapped the cover. "I'll just bet you this was one of your father's. Tomas was always collecting strange old books."

"This was the only one I found up there."

Nelly wasn't listening. She was up and rummaging around in a drawer, mumbling to herself the way she did whenever she was looking for anything. With a triumphant squeal, she turned back to Vlad and dropped a ring of keys on the table. "Your parents gave me copies of all their keys on the off chance they lost any of them. I'll just bet you it's on there."

Vlad sucked down the last of his tea and, shoving two more cookies into his mouth, grabbed the book and keys and headed back upstairs to his bedroom. He flopped on the bed with the book in hand. There were more than a dozen keys on the ring, and Vlad shuffled through the ones he recognized, as there was no use trying them: keys to the house, the garage, the lockbox where Mom had kept things like birth certificates and Social Security cards, the cars. That left ten keys. Vlad slipped the first one in and turned it. Nothing. He moved through them one by one until there was only one key left to try.

The remaining key was longer than the rest, and its tip was shaped like a woman's head. At least, it looked like a woman's head to Vlad. She had round, pudgy cheeks and pursed lips. On her head was a small crown. He placed the tip of the key against the lock.

It was too big.

Cursing under his breath, Vlad tossed the keys onto the bed, running his hand through his hair in frustration. He pulled the book closer and ran a finger along the shape on the cover. The glyph glowed brightly at his touch. Vlad pulled his hand away with a gasp.

The symbol darkened.

Vlad looked from the book to his hand and back, and with a curious eyebrow raised, he placed his palm against the glyph. It flashed, as if charged by his touch. He tried to pull his arm away, but his hand was glued to the spot. Frowning, he pulled again. His hand wouldn't budge. The locks clicked, and as they popped open, the light dimmed and released Vlad's hand. He rubbed his palm, debating whether or not he should look inside when the outside was so bizarre.

Nudging the straps aside, he opened the front cover and was greeted by a line of strange symbols. He flipped through the pages—some had strange drawings of weapons and altars; most were filled with paragraphs of a bizarre symbol language that Vlad couldn't understand. With a sigh, he rolled onto his back.

The book slipped off the bed and made a rather loud thump on the floor. Vlad reached for it, pausing with interest at the page that had fallen open in the book's descent.

In the margin at the bottom were some scribbles that he recognized at once to be his father's handwriting. Vlad ran the tip of his finger along the slanted words and read aloud. "Look to my study. There lie the answers to all that I've hidden." Beneath the script his father had written *Yours in Eternity*. Vlad blinked back tears at the familiar phrase. For as long as he could remember, that was how his father had signed every birthday card, every letter, every book inscription to him. *Yours in Eternity*. His father was speaking to him from the grave.

He read the note over again and curled up on his side, again tracing with his fingertip the words his father had written. His eyelids fluttered closed, and Vlad fell into the deepest sleep he'd had in three years.

9

SNOW AND ASHES

THE GYM WAS DECORATED with several hundred silver and white balloons and enough streamers to wrap around the entire planet twice. Shiny aluminum-foil stars hung from the ceiling. A large white banner draped over the DJ's booth proclaimed in swirling blue script that the students were indeed at Bathory Junior High's Annual Snow Ball. Vlad was leaning up against the wall near the punch bowl, watching two girls giggle excitedly to his left. Henry punched him lightly in the arm. "You could at least be nice to her. I mean, she's not Meredith, but she is your date. Besides, she's pretty cute."

But Vlad didn't want to be nice to Carrie Anderson. He wanted to be nice to Meredith, whom he hadn't seen since winter break. She was currently laughing at something witty that Tom Gaiber had just said. Vlad raised his head up and thumped it against the wall. "I should've stayed home."

Carrie leaned over to Kelly Anbrock, and both girls erupted in another fit of giggles. Henry smiled at Kelly and she blushed. "Hey, Kelly, you wanna dance?"

"Sure." They moved onto the dance floor. Kelly draped her arms around Henry's neck and they turned in slow circles together. On their second turn, Henry gestured to Carrie with his eyes.

Vlad glanced at Meredith, whom Tom was clutching too close for Vlad's comfort. "Carrie—"

"I'd love to!" Carrie dragged him onto the dance floor. She flung her arms around him, and Vlad suddenly remembered what Henry had told him when he'd arranged their dates for the evening. Carrie was a great kisser.

But he didn't reflect long enough to explore how Henry had come by this information.

Vlad placed his hands on her waist and shifted his feet back and forth until they were turning just slightly. He hated dancing. And he didn't especially want to kiss Carrie, but it was better than not having a date at all. Besides, it wasn't like Carrie was a troll or anything. She had sparkling green eyes and curly red hair. Henry was right—she *was* pretty cute.

Tom was laughing so loud that everyone in the gym turned their heads to see what was so funny. Vlad turned his head to look at the far end of the gym behind him, where Tom was looking, but there wasn't anything particularly humorous there—unless you counted the horrific tissue flowers the dance committee had taped to the wall in the shape of a snow-flake. But that was more scary and ridiculous than funny. Vlad turned his head back to Tom, and his heart sank.

Tom was pointing directly at him.

"Hey, goth boy, how much did you have to pay Carrie to dance with you?" Bill was snickering along with Tom. To Vlad's immense surprise, Carrie giggled and pulled away. A few stragglers near Tom and Bill chuckled openly.

But Meredith wasn't laughing anymore.

Vlad straightened his shoulders and gave a sly smile to Tom. "Not a dime. I just offered her tickets to your next ballet recital."

The crowd went silent. Music poured from the DJ's speakers—a heavy bass line that echoed into the gym. Vlad looked at Henry, whose jaw had almost literally hit the floor. Tom's face had turned purple, and Vlad could count the number of veins popping out of his forehead.

Three.

Probably the same number of seconds Vlad had to live once Tom got hold of him.

It was Mike Brennan who broke the silence. He howled with laughter and stepped away from Tom to pat Vlad on the back. Vlad managed a smile but kept his eyes on Tom. It's hard to celebrate when your face is about to be mashed to a pulp.

Henry's laughter followed Mike's, and soon the entire room

was howling—all but Tom, Bill, and Meredith. Carrie rushed into Vlad's arms and planted an unexpected, enthusiastic kiss on his lips. Over her shoulder, Vlad watched as Tom pleaded with Meredith to stay. His begging had apparently fallen on deaf ears, as Meredith yanked her hand away and disappeared out the gym door.

Vlad pulled away from Carrie and took two steps toward the door, but it was too late. Meredith was gone.

Vlad waited until the next day to tell Henry all about his experience with the book and his theories about the strange note left by his father. "What if somebody killed him and Mom and the answers are somewhere in my old house?"

Henry was less than enthusiastic. "Vlad, your parents died three years ago. It was an accident. A horrible, awful accident. Do you really think your dad would've had the foresight to leave you cryptic notes? He probably wrote that for someone else." He was sitting on the edge of Vlad's bed, glancing carefully toward the closed door.

Vlad ran his thumb over the cover of the book. The glyph flickered in response.

"I'm not saying we shouldn't check it out," Henry went on. "Who knows? We might find something. But the odds of your dad knowing he was going to die and that you'd be alive and in possession of his book..." Henry's eyes dropped to the tome in question. "Well, they're not good."

Vlad placed his palm against the glyph. The locks clicked

and opened. "I'm going to my old house to look around. Are you coming or not?"

Henry was watching him with a look of unease. "Whoa . . . how'd you do that?"

"Do what?"

"Your eyes . . ."

Vlad tilted his head, wondering exactly what Henry was talking about. He was about to ask when Henry said, "Just now, when you touched the book, your eyes changed color. They were . . . kind of . . . purple."

Vlad laughed, but stopped when he saw the flicker of fear in Henry's eyes. "Seriously?"

At Henry's nod, Vlad carried the book into the bathroom. He placed his hand on the glyph and watched his reflection. His irises seemed to shift and ripple, like the surface of a pond when broken by a tossed stone. The rippling slowed, then ceased. Vlad's eyes flashed a shade of lavender.

Vlad almost dropped the book. "Whoa!"

Henry was standing behind him. He winced when he saw Vlad's eyes change again. "That's freaky." Henry looked over Vlad's shoulder at the open book. "I thought you promised Nelly you'd stay away from your old house."

"I owe it to my dad to break that promise, Henry. I have to look around at least. What if my dad really did know that he was going to die?" Vlad read his father's note over again and shut the book. He was going to his old house, with or without Henry.

D'Ablo pulled off his leather gloves and tossed them onto the charred floor of Tomas's bedroom. "It's not possible." He looked around the room. It smelled like ashes; it smelled like death.

D'Ablo clucked his tongue and closed his eyes. "Where are you, Tomas? You can't possibly be dead." When he opened his eyes, he noticed a small panel beside the charred bed. He knelt and brushed away the soot with his fingers.

The glyph glowed a cool blue.

A wicked smile crossed D'Ablo's face. "What's this?" He pressed his palm against the glyph, and it glowed brighter before the panel opened inward.

Inside the small compartment were cobwebs, three dead spiders, and a photograph of a boy with black hair. D'Ablo clutched the picture in his hand and frowned. "Well, well. Vladimir Tod. And no sign of your father's beloved journal."

He slid the photo into his pocket and moved to the board-covered window. It would soon be getting light. It was time to leave.

D'Ablo let himself quietly out of the house. His stomach rumbled with hunger, but he ignored it. There was no time to eat, and sleepiness was beginning to overtake him.

When the sun fell once again, he would feed.

Vlad's old house was at the opposite end of town—in a place neither Vlad nor Henry had been in the three years since the accident. Nelly had put the property up for sale twice in that time, but both times Vlad had talked her out of selling it to add to his college fund. Someday, he'd told her, someday he'd have the strength to let the house go. But not yet.

Kind as she was, Nelly had continued to pay the property taxes, kept Bathory's town council pacified, and allowed Vlad time to heal.

He hadn't yet done so.

Vlad paused on the corner and looked down Lugosi Trail. His house was still standing, remaining structurally unharmed, despite the fire. No one could tell Vlad how the fire had started or even how it had been extinguished. Only one room had burned—his parents' bedroom. The fire marshal had brought in several inspectors, but the only conclusion they'd reached was that there had been a brief flash in that room, burning everything and everyone who'd been in it to a crisp, while it had merely smoked and singed the rest of the home's interior.

Vlad could feel Henry's eyes on him, as if waiting for Vlad to burst into tears. Vlad wouldn't. He'd resolved to stop crying in front of people, dealing with his grief on his own in the shadows of his secret space in the belfry of Bathory High. Vlad kept his eyes on the house as they approached. It looked exactly as it had the last time he'd seen it.

The house was an odd, irregular shape—two stories with a three-story tower attached. His bedroom had been at the bottom of the tower. On top of it was his parents' room and on top of that was his dad's study. The exterior of the house was painted gray except for the black gingerbread, which matched the roof's peaks. Atop his father's study was a wrought-iron widow's walk.

Vlad used to play in the backyard at night, only to glance up and spy his parents swaying slowly together to music he couldn't hear from the ground. There might not have been music to dance to at all, but his parents danced anyway. He rubbed the threat of a tear away and reached for the key ring in his pocket.

The door opened easily, and as it swung to the side, Vlad half expected to see his mother behind it, greeting him with a kiss on the forehead and questions about his day. She wasn't there, of course, but her favorite jacket was hanging on the coat tree next to the door. Like everything else in the house, it had been darkened by smoke, but the color showed through the gray.

Henry squeezed his shoulder from behind. "You okay?"

Vlad shook him away and stepped into the house. An acrid smell invaded his nostrils. "We should start in my dad's study."

"Any idea what we're looking for?" Henry stood beside the couch and looked around, a pained expression in his eyes.

"I don't know for sure. In my dad's note, he wrote that the answers were there." Vlad moved through the house, not allowing his eyes to linger on anything for more than a second. Every piece of furniture, every book, every rug, was exactly as it had been the last time he'd seen them. In three years, nothing had been moved. With a heavy heart, Vlad stepped into the passageway that led to the tower and ascended the spiral staircase all the way to the third floor.

Henry followed behind, mumbling under his breath. "Did he mention what the questions were?"

The mahogany door at the end of the hall was locked, but Vlad quickly remedied that with a skeleton key. He stepped in first, with Henry not far behind him, and held his breath as he looked about the small room. His father's enormous desk sat at the center. Framed certificates and artwork lined the walls. A big leather chair was behind the desk, and behind that was his father's suit closet. Vlad sank into the still-soft leather and spun slowly. A small window made of colored glass cast a red glow in the room, painting Henry pink. "My dad loved this chair." Vlad fought, but the tears came anyway. Three years hadn't been long enough to quench them.

Henry squeezed his shoulder. "Come on, Vlad. Let's get this over with."

They searched each drawer, tore through every file, examined the contents of every box, and even combed the desk for secret compartments. By the time they had rummaged through the bottom of the closet, the sun had set and they'd run out of places in Tomas's study to look. If Vlad's father had left the answers here, someone else had already found them. Vlad kicked a box across the room and ran his hand through his hair. "It has to be here somewhere."

"What were you hoping to find, Vlad? The name of your parents' killer scribbled down on a notepad? Typed-out details of who killed them, how, and why? The arsonist's fingerprints documented along with a signed confession? Nothing's here." Henry dropped the file he'd been looking through on the desktop, causing a cloud of dust to rise into the air between them. He took a deep breath and flashed an apologetic glance at Vlad. "All I'm saying is maybe you should leave well enough alone. What if digging through this stuff, nosing around, does nothing but drive you crazy?"

Vlad shook his head. Henry couldn't possibly understand. Vlad thought of replying, but nothing that came to mind could make Henry get how he was feeling. He walked out and made his way downstairs, careful not to even glance at his parents' bedroom door. As he opened the door to his old bedroom, he heard Henry's footfalls behind him. Without looking at him, Vlad said, "You didn't have to come."

Vlad's room was littered with smoke-stained toys that had been important to him at some point in time, though he strained to remember when. On his bed lay an old pair of jeans and, next to it, a crumpled shirt. At the foot of his bed was a lime-green beanbag, and behind it his walk-in closet, where clothes still hung. Everything had been abandoned in the wake of the fire. Vlad reached for the light and chastised himself for forgetting the lack of power. He pulled a small flashlight from his pocket and flipped it on, stepping into the closet. When he reached the back wall, he knelt and loosened the panel there. Inside the wall was a box, which he withdrew and carried to the bed. Henry was watching with guilty interest. "What's that?"

Vlad pulled the lid off and set it next to the box. "It used to be my secret box, where I kept everything that was important to me." He looked inside at the various ticket stubs, photographs, and trinkets, a sad smile finding its way onto his lips.

Henry pulled out a photo of Tomas and looked from Vlad to his father's image and back. "You're just like your dad."

Vlad blinked and looked at Henry with wide eyes. "What did you say?"

He didn't want an answer. In fact, just as "You're ju—" left Henry's mouth again, Vlad bolted out the door and ran as fast as he could back to his father's study. Henry followed close behind. "Where are you going?"

Vlad yanked open the study door and rushed inside. Henry caught the door before it could hit him in the face. "But we already looked here, Vlad."

Vlad opened the closet door and pushed his father's favorite jacket aside. Behind him, Henry was sighing in exasperation. "What are you doing in the closet?"

On the back wall of the closet was a symbol similar to the one that was on the front of his father's book. Vlad reached forward to touch it, and it glowed. Vlad paused. "Do me a favor and touch that symbol."

"I don't see what the point—"

"Just do it, Henry."

Henry slapped his hand against the symbol.

Nothing happened.

It didn't glow, didn't flicker or flash or anything. Vlad reached for it again, and again it glowed. "Must be a vampire thing." Pushing forward, he touched the tips of his fingers to the wood. The glyph glowed even brighter and the panel slid open.

Henry was leaning over his shoulder. "How'd you do that?"

"I have no idea." Vlad peered into the space and withdrew a book, long and thin, with the same symbol on its cover. Beneath it was embossed *The Chronicles of Tomas Tod*. Vlad flipped to the first page in his father's journal and read. *I had never intended to fall in love with Mellina.* Vlad read over his father's handwriting twice more before settling in his father's chair and continuing aloud.

———————◦◦◦———————

JANUARY 13

I had never intended to fall in love with Mellina. She was to be a meal, a taste of human blood, nothing more.

When I found her, she was walking back to her apartment in the blowing January snow. She was alone, buttoned carefully into a thick wool coat with a scarf tied fast around her neck. I could smell her blood, warm and sweet, coursing through her body—as appealing in the cold as I imagine hot chocolate would be to humans. I moved ahead of her and stepped out of the shadows into her path. She paused and looked up at me with her large brown eyes. I'd expected her to scream. But she merely smiled and asked me if I'd like to walk her home.

It was love at first glimpse—something only fairy tales speak of.

I visited her every night for three years, and then, one fine spring day, we wed beneath the sycamore tree in the park not far from her home. Her belly was already full of young Vladimir by that time—an enormous, delightful surprise to us both. But it was also a time of great secrecy, as vampires are forbidden to become entangled in romantic webs with humans.

We decided to flee from the city, away from the watchful eye of Elysia—somewhere safe where we could raise Vlad in peace. On the day we left, as we packed our belongings into her car, I was approached by an old friend. He disagreed with what I was doing, warned me that he couldn't protect me from the council's punishment. And while I believed at that moment and have believed ever since that he was perfectly correct about the danger that surrounded my love affair. I had to leave, to begin life anew with my bride and my son.

And so I did.

Mellina and I stole away to the town of Bathory, where Mellina had grown up. It was much smaller than the city I knew and loved—barely a speck on the map and practically nonexistent as far as the rest of the world was concerned. My wife introduced me to her most cherished friend—a nurse by the name of Nelly—to whom we entrusted my deepest secret. Nelly took the news of my vampiric nature in stride. She was more curious than terrified, and so my secret, Mellina's secret, became Nelly's as well. Not thirty days later, young Vladimir was born in the master bedroom of our new home, with Nelly's careful assistance.

I'd feared Vladimir would be deformed—a punishment for having abandoned ages-old laws and customs. But he was healthy. Pale and ravenous, but healthy. Mellina joked that breast-feeding was out of the question. And oh, how those words made me laugh. I can recall looking at them together—she on the bed, Vladimir swaddled snugly in a white blanket in her arms, one tiny fang protruding from his puckered mouth—and marveling that all I had feared had been wrong. I had a family, and one like no other vampire before me.

Vladimir grew into a healthy, happy child. His hair is black as midnight—so like mine, and his eyes... exquisite. His skin has retained its paleness. He is a thin child—I expect due to the lack of proper nourishment. Oh, he eats well enough—always from the blood Nelly brings home from the hospital. (No one ever notices her thievery, as whole blood "expires" after forty-five days and Nelly only brings home blood that is close enough to that mark that no one is aware it is being stolen and not disposed of.) Despite Nelly's insistence, there is a strong difference between drinking bagged blood and blood from the source. I hear her arguments without countering, as Nelly is human and cannot possibly understand the delicacies of the vampiric palate.

As of this writing, Vlad is two years old and has brought his mother and me more joy than either of us has ever known. He is our light, our life, and I will do all that I can to protect him from the wrath of Elysia.

I plan to rid myself of my mark tomorrow. It's too dangerous to keep, though I cannot remember a time that my wrist was without this black, heavy ink. It will be painful, as it cannot be removed by human means. I must expose it to sunlight until all of Elysia is burned from within me. I wonder what my fellow vampires would think of my decision to remove the tattoo, but it doesn't matter. I will do what I can to protect my family.

The entry ended two-thirds of the way down the yellowed page. Vlad closed the book and hugged it to his chest.

Henry shuffled his feet, apparently uncomfortable over Vlad's discovery. "We should get back. My mom will be wondering where we've been all day." Outside, the sky had turned a rich purple as the sun made its descent.

Vlad followed him out the door. Neither spoke all the way to Henry's house. When they stepped inside, they were greeted by the smell of chocolate and cookie dough. Henry's mom was baking again. Vlad smiled at the flash of apron from the kitchen.

"Hello, boys!" Henry's mom, Matilda, had never failed to greet them with a singsongy voice, full of brightness and cheer. Vlad loved it, but the sound of her voice made Henry's eye twitch. Vlad glanced at Henry, and yep, it was twitching already. But not nearly as much as it did when she referred to Henry as "we."

"Hey, Mom." Henry brushed past her, toward the smell of sugary treats. He was only gone a moment, just long enough for Vlad to exchange smiles with Matilda. When he returned, he handed Vlad a cookie.

Matilda eyed Henry suspiciously. "And where have we been all day, young man?"

Henry's eye twitched again. He lifted one shoulder in a halfhearted shrug. "You know, out and about."

At first she didn't look as though she believed her son was capable of innocence, but then she dried her hands on her apron and smiled warmly. "Well, you boys had better wash up for dinner."

Vlad shot Henry a look, but he was already offering up the usual excuse. "Vlad already ate, Mom." In protest, Vlad's stomach rumbled. Safely tucked inside Vlad's backpack were two bags of blood. It couldn't be easy for Henry to keep Vlad's secret, especially from his family, but he did it anyway.

Some humans were so cool.

Matilda turned back to the kitchen and called over her shoulder, "Honestly, Vladimir, I'm not that terrible a cook. You don't have to eat before you come over."

"He just has a picky appetite, Mom." Henry winked at Vlad and grinned, the tension of the day behind them at last.

Later that night, as Henry lay snoring on his bed, Vlad wriggled out of his sleeping bag and opened his dad's journal. He read with a flashlight until his eyelids felt so heavy that he could barely hold them open anymore, but decided to read just one more entry before giving up the fight against sleep.

———⟶✦⟵———

SEPTEMBER 6

I've just returned from Stokerton, where I found a faded letter nailed to the door of Mellina's long-empty apartment. My old friend wrote, pleading with me to return to Elysia, swearing that all would be well, and promising that he would approach the council himself concerning my crimes. But he lies. He's never had the strength to stand up to the president, let alone plead to the council for the safety of a known criminal. He cannot be trusted.

I told Mellina that I spent the evening on the couch, but I can see in her eyes that she knows I am lying. I cannot bring myself to tell her the truth—that I stole away once more to spy on Elysia—so I shall continue to lie, in order to protect her and Vlad from the curiosity that I cannot contain.

Vlad continues to amaze me with his clever wit and ease of secrecy. Though I find concern in his close friendship with Henry, I do not believe Vlad would risk our way of life by exposing our truth to a human—even one so remarkable as Henry.

Today was Vlad's first day of kindergarten. I resisted enrolling him, but Mellina pleaded with me, and I can refuse her nothing. Mellina will bring his lunches, and Vlad has been strictly forbidden to expose his fangs in front of the humans, but how long our restrictions will hold, I dare not guess. Vlad is a mature boy, no doubt, but he is also a child. A child cannot be expected to behave as adults do.

Vlad returned unscathed from school, but every moment he is away from me, I am saddened. I find the spirit of Elysia within him. He is more than my son. He is my brother in blood.

While I was in Stokerton, I uncovered further notes regarding the Pravus. My studies must be intensified on this matter, and so I will steal away once more to Elysia over the next few weeks so that I can consult the sacred texts. I must act stealthily, lest I become a prisoner of Elysia's council. The texts are in the council's library.

What a chore. Were it not for the tunnel my old friend and I had dug, it would be impossible.

As it is, it shall be a damned, despicable chore that I must steal from my brethren in order to confirm my suspicions concerning my son.

Vlad read the passage again and paused to reflect on the word *Elysia*. He had no idea what it meant, but the tone of his dad's words raised more than a few of the hairs on the back of his neck. His dad had sounded frightened.

Vlad ran his fingers over the scribbled text before pressing his cheek to the page and allowing his eyelids to flutter closed.

He did not dream.

10
A MEETING OF MONSTERS

VLAD WAS RUBBING SUNBLOCK on his face when Henry knocked on the bathroom door. "Be right out." Vlad smeared a bit across his nose until it was all absorbed, then opened the door. Henry was sitting at the foot of his bed, sulking.

"So are you still reading that stupid journal?" Henry glanced over at the journal, which was poking out of Vlad's open backpack.

Vlad grabbed his bag and led the way down the stairs. "It's not stupid."

They walked to school, winding their way through the streets without speaking a word. When they reached Room 6, Henry said, "I hope you haven't forgotten anyone." He nodded toward Meredith, who was exchanging Valentine's gifts with Kara and Melissa.

The classroom looked like Cupid had thrown up all over it.

Vlad cringed at the lace doilies, the pink and red hearts, and the winged infants that dotted the walls. He moved toward his desk and sat down. Mr. Otis entered the room right after Vlad. He wasn't wearing a costume. In fact, he looked pale and rather sickly. He dropped his bag on his desk and took his seat.

Mike Brennan held up one of the fallen paper cupids and piped up from the back of the room. "Hey, Mr. Otis. Is today the day we start studying fairies?"

The class erupted in laughter, but Mr. Otis remained stony. His voice was gruff. "Today will be a free day to work on your presentations."

Vlad relaxed in his seat and lost himself in his father's journal for the better part of an hour. After some time, he came to a curiously short passage and paused.

———— >●< ————

SEPTEMBER 21

A year of studies has convinced me. The Elysian prophecy is being fulfilled in Vlad. He will be a great man, of that there is no doubt.

———— >●< ————

Vlad jumped when Mr. Otis's voice—hoarse, as if he were suffering from a cold—boomed into the room. "That doesn't look like your presentation, Mr. Tod." He gestured for Vlad to come forward, and after giving a heavy sigh, Vlad carried the journal to the teacher's desk. Mr. Otis looked at the cover for a moment and then flipped through the book's pages briefly. He pursed his lips and met Vlad's gaze. "See me after class."

The remaining minutes of class dragged on for just short of an eternity. Mr. Otis alternated between staring blankly at his desk and flipping through pages of Tomas's journal—something that really irritated Vlad. Wrong or not, Vlad deserved a little privacy. But the likelihood was that Mr. Otis wouldn't see the journal as anything but a creative fiction, so he watched the clock tick the time away and let out his irritation with deep, calming breaths.

The bell rang and the class filed out into the hall. Vlad approached Mr. Otis's desk, ready for the lecture that was coming. Through the door, he could see Meredith talking with Henry in the hall. She was twirling a lock of her hair around her index finger and looking from Henry's shoes to his eyes and back. Henry had his hands in his pockets and his trademark grin on his lips. Henry must have said something funny, because Meredith laughed and touched his arm.

Vlad seethed.

Then, as if the flirtatious torture weren't enough, Meredith withdrew a carefully made valentine from her English book and handed it to Henry. Vlad's heart slammed against his ribs like they were iron bars and it was a prisoner trapped within his chest.

Life had a nasty way of being increasingly unfair.

Vlad reached into his backpack and pulled out a pathetic box of chocolates. He scowled at his crooked handwriting. *To Meredith—sweets for the sweet. Vlad.* With a flick of the wrist, he tossed them into the trash can beside Mr. Otis's desk.

Mr. Otis looked from the chocolates to Vlad with a distinct lack of sympathy. "When you are in my class, Vladimir, you will do as I instruct. You will not review materials that have nothing to do with the assigned subject matter. Do I make myself clear?"

Tomas's journal lay open on Mr. Otis's desk. Vlad tore his attention from it and looked his teacher in the eye. "Crystal."

Otis dropped his gaze. His tone softened greatly. "If it's not too personal, Vlad, may I ask why you live with your aunt and not with your parents?"

"My mom and dad..." Vlad swallowed a growing lump in his throat. He rarely spoke to anyone about Tomas and Mellina. And why was Mr. Otis asking about them? "They died three years ago."

Otis shifted in his seat. A great weight seemed to settle on his shoulders and he slouched over his desk. "I'm terribly sorry. How exactly did they die?"

"It was an accident—a house fire." Vlad shifted his weight from one foot to another. "Why do you want to know?"

Otis shook his head, lost in thought. "Tragic. You must miss them very much." His voice caught in his throat in what seemed like empathy. "Were you close to your father?"

That was enough. Vlad pressed his lips together and flashed Mr. Otis a firm look. "Can I have my journal back now, Mr. Otis?"

"But this isn't your journal, Vladimir, not really." Mr. Otis's voice softened further, until it was almost a whisper. He caressed the pages of the journal lovingly before handing it to Vlad. "You should be careful what you believe, Mr. Tod. The world is full of monsters with friendly faces."

Vlad snatched the journal and swung his backpack over his shoulder. His blood was sizzling. Without surprise, Vlad could feel his fangs scraping the inside of his lip. When he reached the door, he paused and turned back, careful to keep his fangs hidden. "Thanks for the advice, Mr. Otis. But I know more about monsters than you can even imagine."

Mr. Otis merely nodded.

As Vlad opened his locker, he looked around for Henry, but didn't see him anywhere. He did, however, see Meredith. She smiled and bounded over to him. "Happy Valentine's Day, Vlad."

Vlad cleared his throat. He was still angry at her for flirting with his best friend, but getting mad at pretty girls is easy; staying mad at them is another story altogether. "Yeah, you too."

"I didn't see you after English, so I left a valentine I made for you with Henry." She raised her hand and twirled one of her perfect brown ringlets around her finger.

Vlad melted into the floor. "Oh...I...I forgot yours at home."

A slight blush tinged her cheeks pink. "It's okay. You don't have to get me anything."

"I already did. It's...it's really nice." The hallway was becoming quickly less populated, which meant there wasn't much time before the bell rang. Vlad managed a smile without blushing too much. "Well, I'd better hurry or I'll be late for math."

Meredith groaned. "Isn't Mr. Harold the worst? I have him fourth period."

Vlad nodded. "Yeah, he's pretty bad."

"See you later, Vlad."

"Yeah." Vlad closed his locker and floated down the hall to Mr. Harold's second-period math class.

Vlad finished reading the journal for the night and marked the page with a paper clip before closing it. Despite Henry's objections, he *had* been learning a lot from his dad's entries lately. He stood and moved his lawn chair closer to one of the belfry's arched windows. The town of Bathory was eerily silent, and the air was charged with a particularly uncomfortable vibe. Even the goth kids had neglected their place on the high school's steps for the evening.

Vlad extinguished the candles and stepped out onto the ledge. He looked over the town, feeling more than just literally above it. In his journal, Tomas had spoken of an entire world populated by vampires. Tomas ranted about a vampire who he thought would come for him and his family, because Tomas had committed the horrendous crime of loving a human and deserting vampirekind. The idea of other vampires sent a chilling thrill through Vlad's veins. It was both terrifying and undeniably exciting. And the journal gave Vlad all the proof he needed to believe his parents had been murdered.

A low, muffled sound that might have been shouting reached Vlad's ear. He turned his head toward the parking lot of the junior high school two blocks over. Two men were arguing loudly. Vlad tucked the journal in his inside jacket pocket and floated down to a nearby oak. Willing his body forward, he bounced gingerly from tree to tree until he stood in the crook of another large oak tree, over the heads of the two arguing men.

Mr. Otis opened the door to his car. His usual smile had been replaced with a sneer. He dropped his bag in the front seat and turned back to the man dressed in black. "This conversation is over."

"Don't speak to me like I'm one of your students, Otis." The man slanted his dark eyes. His words were fog in the cool air. "Where is Tomas?"

Vlad raised a perplexed eyebrow. The man couldn't possibly mean his dad. Walking carefully out onto a branch, Vlad perched on the limb and listened.

"I can't provide you with information I don't have." Otis looked at the ground at his feet and lowered his voice so that

Vlad had to strain to hear him. "The boy will lead me to him. Give him time."

The man in black stepped forward, his body suddenly stiff, anxious. "You've located the Pravus?"

Otis met the man's eyes with a stubborn glance. "I've been in contact with Vladimir, yes."

Vlad leaned so far forward at the mention of his name that he had to steady himself with his hand on another branch or he'd have fallen on Mr. Otis's head. Now *that* would have been an awkward moment.

After a moment of silence, the man placed his arm on the roof of Otis's car and drummed his fingers with a decided lack of patience. "Why are you hiding your thoughts from me, Otis? And why haven't I been able to read the minds of the townspeople? You've found a connection to Tomas after the council has searched for him for fourteen long years, and you haven't informed anyone? Why? What are you up to?"

Otis glanced up at the branch that Vlad was perched on. Vlad held his breath. He couldn't possibly be seen from this distance, especially not with the cover of darkness. Yet Vlad swore he could feel Otis's eyes on him.

After a nerve-rackingly long moment, Otis returned his attention to the man in front of him, but he didn't speak.

The man grabbed Otis by the collar and hissed, "If you gave those people the Tego charm to block my telepathy—"

Otis laughed, but his posture suggested he was ready to defend himself if need be. "You worry too much. I'm on your side. Remember? I want to find Tomas just as much as you do."

The man relaxed his grip on Otis's collar and took a step back. "Then explain to me what's going on here."

Otis smiled, his eyes chastising. "Have you considered that Tomas may have given the Tego charm to any number of Bathory citizens? He is trying to elude us, after all."

The man searched Otis's eyes and nodded. "I suppose it's possible."

A tingling sensation had begun at Vlad's toes and was spreading upward. His foot had fallen asleep. He sat, allowing his numb foot time to stop tingling. The branch creaked softly beneath him.

The man's eyes darted to the tree Vlad was sitting in. Once again, Vlad didn't breathe. "Did you hear something?"

Otis placed a hand on the man's shoulder and directed him back to the sidewalk. "Being away from Elysia is making you paranoid, D'Ablo. Go home. Get some rest. When I locate Tomas, I'll contact you."

After D'Ablo had disappeared down the street, Otis turned and walked back to the tree. He looked up at the branch of the large oak, his eyes searching.

From the bushes near the sidewalk, Vlad breathed a very tense, very quiet sigh of relief.

11
Mr. Otis Comes to Dinner

VAMPIRES DRINK BLOOD, SLEEP IN coffins, and fear garlic."
Mr. Otis stood in front of the class, dressed in a black suit
and a cheap vinyl cape not so different from the one Vlad had
worn on Halloween. Leaning against the desk, he looked at
Vlad with a curious glint in his eye and smiled before turning
toward the chalkboard, where he'd taped various artists' inter-
pretations of vampires over the centuries. Vlad paid special
attention to the Hungarian countess and the Transylvanian
prince. Were they real vampires, too? Relatives of his?

Mr. Otis turned back to the class and stared at him intently.
Vlad shifted in his seat. Several of his classmates looked from
their teacher to Vlad. Mr. Otis blinked, awakening from whatever dreamland had occupied his mind for a minute. "Vlad, I
want you to help me with something before you give your
oral presentation." His hand disappeared into one of the desk

drawers, and he retrieved a plastic container, its lid tightly sealed. He held it out.

With a quick glance at Meredith, Vlad left his seat for the front of the class. He took the container and looked expectantly at his teacher. Mr. Otis seemed to be holding his breath, but then he spoke, his voice a low, almost growling whisper. "Please pass the garlic cloves out to the rest of the class, Vladimir."

Vlad looked at the container in his hands. All that stood between him and one of the deadliest herbs known to vampirekind was an eighth of an inch of mustard-yellow plastic.

"I can't." He held the container out to Mr. Otis, who tilted his head and crossed his arms stubbornly in front of him.

"Why not?" Mr. Otis, arms crossed, was tapping one finger against his biceps and watching the container in Vlad's hand with seeming indifference.

Vlad set the container on Mr. Otis's desk. "I'm allergic to garlic. If you don't believe me, check with the office. They have it on file." He shrugged, ignoring the scoffs of some of his classmates.

Mr. Otis paused for a moment, then returned the container to his desk drawer and glanced up at the clock before turning back to Vlad. "All right, then. Let's carry on with your oral presentation on what it's like to be a vampire." He raised his eyebrow. There had been no question in his tone, no suggestion of what it *must be like*. Mr. Otis had omitted those things because there was no question in his mind.

He knew Vlad's secret.

Vlad's legs felt like jelly. His insides had cooled to the point that it seemed his vocal cords were frozen and unable to make a mere utterance.

Vlad focused on pushing into Mr. Otis's thoughts. A blurry image began to form at the forefront of his mind. It was red— red like blood. The feeling that accompanied it was fear. Mr. Otis's crisp voice shook Vlad from his trance. "Vlad. Please continue with your presentation."

Vlad cleared his throat and slowly turned to face the rest of the class. He looked back at his empty desk and wished that he was there before clearing his throat needlessly again. "My name is Vladimir Tod, and I'm . . . I'm a vampire." His ears suddenly felt very warm. He glanced at Mr. Otis, who gestured for him to continue. Vlad's mind went blank. He couldn't remember what he'd previously written on the subject.

Mr. Otis looked irritated. The rest of the class shifted listlessly.

Vlad decided to wing it. "It's not easy, being a bloodsucking creature of the night. If I go out without my sunblock, I'll likely burst into flames." Meredith chuckled. She wasn't alone. Suddenly Vlad didn't feel quite so mortified.

"Aside from characters in books and stories that I can't prove to be true, I'm pretty sure I'm the only vampire left. It's kind of lonely, but at least I don't have to wait in long lines at the blood bank." Vlad smiled. To his immense surprise, he was enjoying this. "If I concentrate, I can make my body float, and sometimes I can read people's thoughts. But for the most part, being a vampire bites."

The class erupted in applause. Even Mr. Otis gave a smile.

Vlad turned back to his seat, and as he walked away, he threw Mr. Otis another glance. His teacher reached for his coffee cup, his sleeve pulling up enough to reveal the hint of a tattoo on the inside of his wrist. The ink was thick and black.

Vlad gasped aloud. It looked a lot like the symbol that had been carved into Mr. Craig's porch—the one that had been haunting him for months. The only difference was that the lines were slanting in the opposite direction.

The bell rang its shrill tone, pronouncing school officially over. Vlad gathered his books and bolted from the classroom without so much as a glance at Mr. Otis.

Henry was waiting on the steps outside. His backpack was slung over one shoulder, and one of his thumbs was threaded through a belt loop on his jeans. He smiled at Vlad, but his smile quickly melted as Vlad moved closer. "What's wrong? You look pale."

Though he normally laughed at Henry's puns, Vlad ignored the quip and grabbed a handful of Henry's shirt. "I think Mr. Otis killed my parents."

Henry gaped at him.

Vlad let go of his shirt and leaned in close. He glanced over his shoulder and back at Henry. "And Mr. Craig, too."

Regaining his composure a bit, Henry said, "But Vlad, we don't even know for sure if Mr. Craig is dead or not. That's crazy."

On the walk home, Vlad spilled almost all of it, outlining in detail his visit to Mr. Craig's house, seeing Otis's top hat there and the mysterious symbol that he'd seen in four other places—and the similar mark on the inner wrist of Mr. Otis. He told Henry about his dad's mention of a tattoo that he'd planned to remove with sunlight and of the conversation he'd overheard between Otis and a man dressed entirely in black, who went by the name D'Ablo.

Henry shook his head, but didn't discount Vlad's theories. "So what is he, some kind of gang member? A mob assassin?"

Vlad shook his head and brushed the wisp of bangs from his eyes. "He's a vampire."

Henry laughed, but stopped when he looked at Vlad. "You can't be serious."

"I'm dead serious." Vlad slowed his steps as they neared his house. He glanced at the house and wondered whether Nelly was home yet. "I think he's going to try to hurt me. In Dad's journal, he said—"

"Vlad, that's nuts. I mean, I know you miss your parents and Mr. Craig, but accusing your teacher of being a vampire? That sucks, dude." Henry smirked, pleased at the new pun. All traces of a smile faded when Vlad failed to laugh. "Even if he is a vampire—and I'm not saying for sure he's not—if he were going to hurt you, wouldn't he have done it by now?"

"Not if he thinks he needs me to locate my dad."

"But your dad is—"

"I know, Henry! I was the one who found them!" Vlad was fuming. He tightened his grip on his backpack's strap and turned toward his house. "Dead. My parents are dead. Why do people keep reminding me?" Henry opened his mouth to answer, but Vlad quickened his pace and slammed the front door of his house behind him.

Vlad threw the journal across the room, sending the lamp on the end table crashing to the floor. Then he bolted back outside. "Henry?"

Henry just looked at him. His eyes were full of hurt.

So were Vlad's. "You believe me, don't you?"

Henry examined the hole in Vlad's shoe before meeting his eyes. "I believe you're scared. And there has to be some reason for it. So . . . sure. Why not vampires?"

"In my dad's journal, he talks about a whole world of vampires, entire cities populated by them. They couldn't all have vanished, could they?"

Vlad must have looked terrified, because Henry lowered his voice and gave him a reassuring nod. "It's not impossible to believe other vampires are out there. And they might be horrible people. You could be right. But don't go freaking out over something we can't prove yet. We'll find out what's going on, Vlad. Just . . . be careful." With another nod, Henry walked off.

Vlad looked up at his house and let out a groan. He'd completely forgotten that this was the night Mr. Otis was coming over for dinner. He let his backpack slip from his shoulder and lugged it into the house.

After tossing his backpack and jacket into his bedroom, Vlad changed his shirt and headed back downstairs. He heated a bag of blood in the microwave and bit into it, then sucked the sweet, warm juices into his mouth and rolled them around on his tongue before swallowing.

Vlad had once seen a book at the mall called *Bloodsucking Fiends*. He didn't remember the author or even what the book was about, apart from its vampire theme, but he found himself mulling over that description of his species and wondered whether people would refer to him as a fiend if they ever found out about him. The thought bothered him at first, but after a while he became drawn to the term. He already sucked blood; he might as well have a cool title like *fiend* to go with it.

Vlad rounded the stairs just as Nelly was shutting the front door with her heel. Her arms were full of grocery bags. "What happened to the lamp?"

"Amenti knocked it over."

The pudgy black cat meowed her protest.

Nelly shook her head at Vlad's shirt. "You're not wearing that."

Vlad looked down at his black T-shirt and the crimson letters that dripped down his chest, mimicking blood. It read VAMPIRES SUCK—Henry's gift to him last Christmas. Vlad sucked some blood off his thumb. "What? I like this shirt."

Nelly gave him that you've-got-to-be-kidding-me-if-you-think-I'm-giving-in-on-this-one look and carried the bags into the kitchen. Vlad followed her. "What's for dinner?"

She was pulling fresh hamburger out of one bag, and Vlad stared at the red juices that clung to the plastic wrap around the meat. "Meat loaf. Will you be okay faking through a meal? I know you don't like swallowing cooked meat, but—"

"No big deal, Aunt Nelly. You act like I haven't been pretending to be normal my entire life." He raised the corner of his mouth in a half smile, pulled the eggs and rice from a bag, and set them on the counter.

Nelly gave him a matter-of-fact nod. "Pretending to be *human*. You *are* normal, Vladimir. A perfectly normal, healthy teenage vampire. Some people are vegetarians, you drink blood—it's not weird or bizarre or abnormal in the least. You're just different from the rest of this town." She set the hamburger next to the eggs and sighed. "I do worry how they'd react if they learned about you. People fear what they can't understand and harm what they fear."

Nelly was right, of course. And Vlad would go on pretending to be something he was not until the world was safe for him to stop ... which would be never, as Vlad saw it. He watched Nelly putting the groceries away and wondered why she'd asked Mr. Otis over for dinner. He was about to ask when the curious idea entered his mind to simply steal his way into her thoughts and see. He concentrated hard and pushed with his mind.

Nelly pressed her palm against her forehead. "I have the worst headache."

Vlad frowned and pushed again with his mind, but nothing happened. Nelly reached for some ibuprofen on the counter and popped two of them into her mouth, then gave Vlad a curious glance. "Are you nervous about having your teacher over?"

"*Substitute* teacher." Vlad ran a finger along the side of the hamburger packet and licked it. He could feel the pressure of his fangs elongating and was tempted to let them remain in plain view during Mr. Otis's visit. Maybe a close encounter with another bloodsucking fiend would shake any information Mr. Otis had out of him. "They still haven't found Mr. Craig."

Nelly shook her head. "I wonder if they ever will. That poor man."

Vlad reached out and covered Nelly's hand with his own. "Aunt Nelly? I kind of need to talk to you about Mr. Otis."

He told her everything: about the book, Otis's hat, Tomas's journal, Otis's tattoo. When he finished, she patted him on the shoulder. "You've been under a ridiculous amount of stress, Vladimir. I'm not surprised you're seeing vampires everywhere. Why, the other day I thought I saw—"

"Not everywhere. Just in my English class." He pulled out the slip of paper he had drawn from Otis's hat weeks before—the one that had read *werewolf* and now read *vampire*.

Nelly read Mr. Otis's horrible handwriting and sighed. "Sweetheart, we're all worried about Mr. Craig. But that's no reason to dislike Mr. Otis. Give him a chance." Giving his shoulder a squeeze, she clapped her hands together, as if signifying some momentous decision. "I'd better get started or dinner will never be ready in time."

Vlad stepped back, stunned that his aunt didn't believe him or even take his concerns seriously. But there was no point in arguing. He'd just have to whittle some hard evidence out of Mr. Otis tonight. Then Nelly and Henry would have to believe him.

Vlad touched one of his fangs with the tip of his finger and shivered as the sharp enamel slipped into his skin. He sucked the blood for a moment and shrugged at Nelly's concerned gaze. She was going to go on looking at him like that forever if he didn't say anything to put her fears at rest. He forced a smile. "Want help with dinner?"

Vlad helped her pull out bowls and pans, crack open eggs, and drizzle their gooey insides into a big glass bowl. He watched Nelly mush the rice and meat together, his thoughts never far away from that tattoo on Mr. Otis's wrist. It was so like the symbol on the porch. It had to be a curse of some kind, or something used by vampires to identify their kill. Vlad's thoughts turned to the black cylinder, and the symbol engraved at the bottom. He wasn't sure how that fit in, but it was clear to Vlad that someone had reached Tomas before D'Ablo could. And that someone was Mr. Otis.

Nelly slid the meat loaf into the oven. She set the timer for an hour, wiped off the counter with a damp rag, and washed her hands. Vlad frowned at the waste of blood as she sopped it up into the dishcloth. He'd been hungrier lately than he usually was—something he attributed to stress and Nelly attributed to hormones. With a tug, she opened the chest freezer and tossed him another bag of blood before slipping upstairs to change.

Vlad bit into the bag, forgoing the microwave, and drank the blood cold, then settled in front of the television. Nothing good was on, but he wasn't in the mood to watch anyway. He was dreading the inevitable arrival of their dinner guest and pondering the possible reasons Mr. Otis would have to kill his favorite teacher.

The doorbell rang.

Vlad raced to the door. He could see the outline of Mr. Otis standing on the porch, no doubt plotting the demise of an innocent boy and his far-too-trusting guardian.

A hand squeezed his shoulder and he jumped. Nelly wrinkled her forehead. "Let him in, Vladimir. Don't be rude."

Vlad swallowed the lump in his throat. He had to think fast. "I think I have the flu. Can't we invite Mr. Otis over some other time?"

Nelly touched the back of her hand to his forehead and looked him over before shaking her head. "Vladimir, you do not have the flu. You can't get the flu, remember? You're just nervous. I don't know a kid on this planet who wants his teacher over for dinner. I promise we won't talk about school, okay?" She opened the door.

Mr. Otis smiled brightly. To Vlad's horror, Otis was once again wearing his top hat. "Good evening, Nelly ... Vlad. Thank you for inviting me."

Nelly smiled back. "We're happy to have you, Otis. I hope you like meat loaf." She led him into the dining room and Vlad remained by the door, looking out at the setting sun with longing. He'd rather be anywhere than here at any time but this. He kicked the door closed and went back to watching TV.

Nelly's voice floated in from the dining room. "Vlad tells me you taught mythology in Stokerton before taking the position here in Bathory."

Otis said, "Oh yes. Quite enjoyed it, too. Not to say I'm not enjoying this school. I couldn't ask for better students."

There was the clinking of dishes as they were moved about. Nelly must have been setting the table. "Why the move, if you don't mind me asking?"

Otis paused for a long time, and Vlad wondered if he'd ever reply. Not that he cared, but still, the silence was unnerving. Otis cleared his throat. "To be honest, I needed a change in scenery."

Ten minutes into a rerun of *Buffy the Vampire Slayer*, Nelly called from the dining room, "Vlad, dinner's nearly ready."

He pushed the button on the remote and the screen went blank. Vlad didn't stir from his chair. The prospect of dinner with the man who'd likely stolen Vlad's parents and teacher from him was enough to sink him into an angry bout of depression.

Nelly came in from the dining room, that look of concern once more wrinkling her brow. "Everything okay?"

Vlad blinked at her. He kept his voice low so their guest couldn't hear. "Do I have to eat dinner with him?"

"You most certainly do. Now go make nice with our guest while I finish making the biscuits." Her eyes were filled with kind understanding. Vlad wanted to shake her, to hide her away from this monster, but what good would it do? Instead, he slouched into the dining room.

"Everything all right?" Mr. Otis was sitting at the table. He'd removed his hat and overcoat and was watching Vlad with an intensity that made Vlad's stomach flip.

Vlad pressed his lips together hard and slowed his steps. No, everything was not all right. It hadn't been for over three years. Ever since Mr. Otis had taken away almost everything that was important to him.

Behind him, Aunt Nelly's voice was cheerful and supportive. "Vlad's just nervous about having his teacher over."

Vlad slumped down in his seat and muttered, "*Substitute* teacher."

Mr. Otis kept his eyes on Vlad. "No need to be nervous, Vladimir. I'm looking forward to getting closer to you and your lovely aunt."

Nelly smiled and disappeared into the kitchen.

"I'm sure you are." Vlad glared.

Mr. Otis cleared his throat.

Vlad continued to glare.

Mr. Otis cleared his throat again. "I enjoyed your oral report today, Vlad. It showed an enormous gift for creative thinking."

Vlad snorted and rearranged his silverware. "Yeah, well, that's me. I love to tell a good story."

"I'm sure we can agree that all stories are embedded with a grain of truth. Wouldn't you say?" Mr. Otis leaned back in his chair and looked toward the kitchen, where Nelly was pulling biscuits out of the oven.

Vlad met his gaze and held it for a moment. The air in the room was growing increasingly thick. "I guess."

Mr. Otis folded his hands together and regarded Vlad with a grim smile. "I'm also sure we can agree that the existence of vampires is little more than a fairy tale. Can't we?"

"What are you driving at, *Mister* Otis?"

Otis paused, as if gathering his thoughts, and then said, "I wanted to discuss your father's journal with you."

"That's none of your business."

"I believe it is."

"Well, pardon the pun, Mr. Otis, but you can bite me." Vlad slammed his fork on the table. "That was your real reason for coming over tonight. Wasn't it?"

Mr. Otis relaxed back in his seat, his expression genuinely surprised. He clucked his tongue. "My, my. It seems my secret is out. You *are* a smart lad."

Nelly entered the room, carrying a basket of steaming biscuits. "Everything okay in here?"

Otis smiled. Vlad scowled.

Nelly looked from one to the other. "I thought I heard a noise."

"No need for concern, Nelly. Vlad merely dropped his silverware on the table by accident. Didn't you, Vladimir?" Otis raised an eyebrow. His smile looked crooked and threatening.

Vlad sat stony-faced. He remained that way for the rest of the meal, listening to the conversation and moving bits of food around his plate without eating. Nelly kept giving him chastising glances, but Vlad ignored her. After Otis had complimented her on her talent in the kitchen, Nelly's eyes twinkled, reminding Vlad of his mom for a moment. It was strange how their mannerisms could be so alike at times, despite the lack of relation between them. "I'd better freshen up. Vlad, you can clear the table."

She slipped upstairs, and Otis smiled after her. "You have a remarkable aunt. It would be a shame if anything were to happen to either of you."

The pressure in Vlad's gums was immediate and intense. His fangs were growing out of both hunger and anger. "Get out."

"Pardon me?"

"Get out of my house, right now. And don't come back."

Mr. Otis showed not even a hint of upset. Nelly walked back into the room and, to Vlad's surprise, Mr. Otis smiled pleasantly. "I should be going. Would you mind if I washed up first?"

Nelly seemed disappointed by his abrupt departure. "Not at all. Upstairs, second door on the left."

After Otis had gone, Nelly leaned against the doorjamb. "What did you do?"

Vlad's eyes grew wide. "Nothing!"

"Well, is there something you want to talk about?"

Vlad ran his tongue along the sharp points of his teeth. "Not really."

"Are you okay?"

"I'm fine." But Vlad wasn't fine. He needed to be alone, to figure out what he was supposed to do to stand against a vampire who was not only much bigger than he was, but had a habit of killing people. Vlad ran up the stairs to his room. He closed his hand over the doorknob, but stopped when he heard a noise on the other side of the door. A scratching noise, like claws against wood. Vlad cracked open the door. Mr. Otis was standing in front of his dresser, his back to Vlad, hunched over Vlad's top drawer. The scratching noise paused, and Vlad shrank back as Mr. Otis raised his head, listening. Vlad stepped back and into the bathroom to hide. He watched Mr. Otis leave his bedroom and walk down the stairs.

Vlad stepped out of the bathroom and crossed the room to his dresser. Inside his chest his heart was rattling in a nervous spasm. He pulled open the drawer, but nothing looked out of place. Socks, boxers, belts, his secret box. He was sliding the drawer closed again, a perplexed wrinkle on his brow, when his eyes widened at the sight of his secret box. It had been a gift from his father when he was only four years old, and Vlad's most prized possession before he found the journal. Clutching the box, Vlad held it up and looked at the bottom. The shape of Mr. Otis's tattoo was carved into it.

Vlad almost dropped the box, but then squeezed his hand around it and returned it to the drawer. He left the room and crossed the library, making sure to stand in the shadows at the top of the stairs, where Nelly and Mr. Otis wouldn't notice his presence. He watched them at the front door. Nelly handed Otis's top hat to him and smiled. "It was lovely having you, Otis. I hope we can do this again sometime."

"It would be my pleasure." Mr. Otis put his hat on and, as he was slipping on his overcoat, said, "It was enlightening speaking with you, Vladimir." He looked up the stairs and met Vlad's eyes. "I'll see you in class tomorrow."

Vlad froze.

"By the way ... I love your shirt." Mr. Otis winked at Vlad and disappeared out the front door.

12
MR. CRAIG

VLAD GRIPPED THE HANDLE of his backpack and pulled, sliding it along the floor behind him until he reached the top of the stairs. Nelly stood at the bottom, looking up at him with a curious glint in her eyes. "You look pale."

Vlad began his descent. The book bag thumped loudly against each step as he moved down them. "I always look pale."

"Yes, but today you look positively cadaverous." She touched his forehead with the back of her hand. "Are you feeling all right?"

Vlad pushed her hand away. "Why do you always do that? I don't get fevers, remember?"

"Must be force of habit from the hospital. Sorry, grouch."

"I'm sorry, Aunt Nelly. You're right. I'm not feeling very well today." In fact, he was feeling terrible, though it couldn't be attributed to any known bacterium floating around in the air. According to his dad's journal, vampires had been through some of the worst epidemics in history. And apparently, during the days of the Black Plague, their biggest complaint had been rotten "food."

"Maybe you should stay home today." She gave a nod and headed for the door. "Get some rest. I'm working a double shift, so I'll be late tonight, but I'll call later to check on you."

Vlad sat his backpack on the bottom step. He was feeling better already. "Hey, before you go, have you ever seen anything like this?" He dug around in his backpack and pulled out a notebook, hastily flipping to the page where he'd scribbled the symbol with the slanted lines and parentheses. "This here."

Nelly squinted over her glasses. "Why, yes. It looks remarkably like Tomas's tattoo. Where did you see it?"

"In a book I read." Vlad wrinkled his forehead and held the notebook closer for inspection. "I don't remember Dad having a tattoo."

"Oh yes. It was thick black ink and right here." She pointed to the inside of her left wrist. "He had it removed when you were a baby. I think I have pictures." Before Vlad could say more, Nelly walked off in the direction of the living room and returned a moment later with a handful of snapshots. She spread them out on the small table near the door. Her eyes filled with sadness as she looked at a picture of her best friend's family—Vlad just a baby then and snuggling close to his mother for comfort. Vlad turned his head, unable to handle the pain the pictures brought. Nelly pointed to Tomas's wrist in one picture. "You can see the tattoo in this one."

Vlad plucked the picture from the table and eyed his dad's tattoo closely. It was an exact copy of the symbol he'd seen in the book, on the porch. "I remember he had a scar there. He told me it was from an accident he had when he was a kid."

When he looked at Nelly, her expression had changed. Her face had become gray, the concerned crease in her brow deepening. She brushed away tears. "Vlad, did I ever tell you about my dog—Gilbert?"

Vlad blinked, unsure where her question was coming from and, more importantly, where it was going.

"Gilbert was a fine dog. No special breed or even particularly attractive, but he'd fetch anything I threw for him, and he slept at the foot of my bed from the time I was five until I was about your age. Then, one night, Gilbert disappeared. I spent months looking for him and cried every night he was gone, hung posters all over the town offering a reward. I lost sleep searching for him, let my grades slip. It really took over my life, looking for that dog. Finally, my father sat me down and told me that he'd taken Gilbert out to the woods behind our house and shot him." She blinked away another tear and patted Vlad on the shoulder, comforting him when, clearly, she was the one in need of comforting.

"Oh, my father wasn't a monster or anything, but it turned out that Gilbert had a very painful bone disease, so my father put him down. To this day, I can't think of my father the same way. Every sweet memory I have is soured by what he did to my dog."

She slung her purse over her arm and looked pointedly at Vlad. "All I'm saying is that you should be grateful that there are some things you don't know about your father, and that sometimes it's best to leave well enough alone."

After she closed the door behind her, Vlad lugged the journal and the large book with the glyph and locks out of his backpack and carried them over to the coffee table. He thumbed through the journal for a few moments before flipping to the final entry, dated the day before his parents died.

———>•<———

NOVEMBER 18

The council is closing in. I am tempted to flee Bathory for the safety of Siberia, but Mellina is not aware of the potential danger we are in, nor is Vlad, and I refuse to educate them in the midst of such a difficult journey. So we shall remain here and I will do whatever is necessary in order to protect them. No matter the cost, Vlad must be preserved.

I have stored several items in Nelly's attic for lack of space in our own. One of them I hope will be of great use to Vladimir as he grows older. It is the Compendium of Conscientia, a book handed down from vampire to vampire since the beginning of our age. Everything he needs to know about our history, our prophecies, and our ways is in this book. It is crucial that Vlad memorize Elysian code and study this text at great length.

I will begin teaching him the code later this week after his tenth birthday celebration. Tonight, I am very weary and must rest. Sometimes I am astonished at how well I've adapted to sleeping at night. If the nightmares of late would cease, I would actually look forward to my head hitting the pillow.

I was foolish in stealing the Lucis during my latest Elysia break-in. It alerted them to my presence, for who would want the tool but me? Should they come for me— tonight, tomorrow, whenever—I will surrender myself to the council's will in exchange for the safety of my family.

But I will not run from them anymore.

———⟫●⟪———

Vlad closed the cover and ran his fingers over his father's name.

Shaking off the sadness, he turned on the television. Nothing was on . . . well, nothing good anyway, but he left the TV on to fill the house with noise and opened the book, flipping to the pyramid of symbols. Vlad traced the outline of his father's tattoo with his fingernail and half listened to the news reporter on Channel 5 who was droning on about some car accident that was blocking an exit on the freeway.

A woman's voice broke in, catching Vlad's interest. "Thank you, Ted. And in other news, a body has been discovered near

Requiem Ravine and is believed to be the remains of a missing Bathory Junior High teacher." Vlad sat up and grabbed the remote, pressing the volume button until the television couldn't blare any louder. "John Craig had been missing for several months when local police pulled his body from the ravine. Police are baffled as to the cause of death, but speculate that an animal may be responsible. Mr. Craig was thirty-four years old. Could a wild dog be running rampant in the streets of Bathory? Although the local police assure us that this has not been proven, this reporter believes it to be a very real, very scary possibility. And now here's Terrance with the weather." Vlad clicked the television off and sank back into the cushions of the couch.

Mr. Craig was dead.

Deceased, croaked, departed, shuffled off his mortal coil, bought the farm, slain, fallen, bit the big one, dead as a doornail, gone, out of business, late, lifeless, taking a dirt nap, kaput, worm food, cashed in his chips, finished, lapsed, pushing up daisies, terminated, inanimate, kicked the bucket, past his expiration date, nonliving, checked out, left the building, bitten the dust, passed away, passed on, isn't-coming-back-for-the-sequel dead.

Killed by a vampire—Vlad was almost sure.

Late last night, in Tomas's journal, Vlad had read about Elysia, of tales of camaraderie and celebration, of familial ties, of being bound by blood. Vlad had found himself longing to encounter those of his own kind, to travel to the streets of

Elysia—that faraway vampire world, but after a while it seemed more of a fairy tale than anything else.

Like Santa Claus and the Tooth Fairy, only with fangs.

But the presence of Mr. Otis had proven quite different from the images Vlad's imagination had conjured up. He felt terribly threatened by Otis's presence. And who was that D'Ablo guy? Another vampire? Were vampires all over Bathory now, hunting for Vlad? And hadn't any of them thought to pick up a phone book? Bathory was populated by fewer than two thousand people, for crying out loud. If Mr. Otis was planning on killing him, why hadn't he done it last night after dinner? Why the games?

If Mr. Otis were from Elysia, why had he killed Tomas? Was Vlad's dad a criminal? And what did that make Vlad? Why was Otis stalking him? He couldn't have broken the law. He'd never even been to Elysia. Vlad shivered. Maybe he wouldn't belong there, either. Maybe no matter where he went, he'd be a freak.

The doorbell rang, shaking Vlad from his daze.

Vlad pulled open the front door and froze. Mr. Otis tipped his top hat slightly, holding Vlad's gaze with his serious eyes. "I was disappointed not to find you in class today, Vladimir." His cheeks looked pale and gaunt, as if he hadn't eaten in some time.

Vlad pursed his lips and looked at his feet. He was tempted to slam the door in Mr. Otis's face and slap the dead bolt until it clicked, but old habits die hard, so instead he stood there and quietly waited for his teacher to finish so he could get on with his life.

"I have an urgent matter to discuss with you, Vlad. I'm afraid it can't wait." Mr. Otis pressed against the door, but Vlad shoved his shoulder against the wood, leaving merely a foot of air between the door and the jamb. His teacher's face was inches from his own. "Mind if I come in for a snack? I'm sure you have something around the house that will appeal to my particular appetite."

Feeling the hairs rise on the back of his neck, Vlad shot his teacher a look fueled by betrayal. "Didn't anybody ever tell you it's not nice to threaten your students?"

"Do you feel threatened by me?" Otis nudged the door forward another inch, as if demonstrating that Vlad's strength wasn't an obstacle for him. "That's not my intent. I just want to get close to you, Vladimir."

Vlad relinquished his hold on the door. He was shaking in his shoes, but he couldn't let Mr. Otis know that. He squeezed his fists tight against his jeans, ready for whatever Otis had in mind.

The corner of Otis's mouth rose, and for a second, Vlad could just make out the hint of a fang. "Let me in, Vlad. Don't make this difficult."

"Don't make what difficult?" The porch boards squeaked as Henry approached, a concerned look on his face.

Mr. Otis looked back and forth between the boys and then glanced behind him, as if weighing his options. Without a word, he turned and stepped off the porch, pausing momentarily before continuing his exit.

Vlad breathed a nervous sigh of relief. "Oh, man. I'm screwed, Henry. I'm totally screwed."

They went upstairs. Henry told Vlad about school getting cut short because of Mr. Craig's body being found, and Vlad told Henry all about last night's dinner. Henry gave him a playful smack on the shoulder. "So you're saying your teacher sucks."

Vlad brushed his bangs out of his eyes and snickered. "That's what I've *been* saying. I mean, he admitted it, Henry. He all but told me he's a vampire."

Henry led the way down the stairs and out the front door. They both kept their eyes alert for any sign of Mr. Otis. When they reached Henry's porch, Henry squinted up at the sun. "I wonder how he keeps from frying in the daylight."

Vlad shrugged. "Maybe he uses sunblock, too. Or maybe he's half human like me."

"Maybe his soul's so dark that even the sun won't touch him." Henry's tone was serious, so Vlad didn't laugh. Instead, he looked quizzically at his friend as he tossed his bag onto the porch. Henry dropped his bag beside Vlad's. "I mean, what kind of a guy stalks teenagers?"

"Not teenagers, man. Me. He's after me." Vlad shivered at the thought of being Mr. Otis's next meal. He suddenly understood why Henry had avoided him for several days after he'd drunk Henry's blood. It made his stomach churn with queasiness. "Hey, Henry?"

"Yeah?"

"I'm sorry about biting you when we were eight."

"No problem. Just stay away from the cat or Mom will throw a fit."

13
Bound by Blood

OTHING COULD CONVINCE AUNT NELLY to let Vlad stay
home for the duration of the school year, which just goes
to prove that parents and guardians don't care if they're sending you to face bloodthirsty monsters, so long as you get a B
in English.

Mr. Otis stood in front of the class. His eyes were still red
from the touching ceremony the school had given in the gym
in honor of Mr. Craig. He hadn't uttered a word or offered so
much as a glance at Vlad in the weeks since their conversation on Vlad's porch. When he finally spoke, his voice cracked
on the first word. "Thank you all for turning in such wonderful
essay papers. I have graded them, and as today is an early-
release day in honor of Mr. Craig's passing, you may pick them
up on your way out the door. Have a safe weekend, ladies and
gentlemen."

Vlad shoved his notebook into his backpack and zipped it

closed. On his way past Mr. Otis's desk, he snatched his paper off the pile and left the classroom, scanning Mr. Otis's various red scribbles as he walked. He'd gotten an A, which only proved that Vlad was excellent at writing from the point of view of a vampire and horrible at figuring out just how much it would cost to get from New York to Los Angeles if gasoline cost $2.35 a gallon and the car he was driving got twenty-six miles to the gallon.

Then Vlad glanced at the words scrawled at the bottom of the last page. He gasped. *I know your secret,* Mr. Otis had written. *I know you're a vampire.*

Vlad almost jumped out of his skin when a hand touched his shoulder. He turned to face Mr. Otis. "I must speak with you in private, Vlad."

Vlad did the same thing he'd done in the sixth grade when Nelly asked him who'd broken Mr. Snelgrove's window. He denied any knowledge pertaining to current events. "Look, if this is about the punctuation test—"

Mr. Otis held up a hand and hissed, "You know what it's about. We're going for a little walk, you and me."

"I."

Mr. Otis's stern brow furrowed. "Excuse me?"

"We're going for a little walk, you and I." Vlad glanced at the double doors. They were only ten feet from him. He looked at Mr. Otis and shrugged. "Honestly, you're supposed to be an English teacher. Besides, I don't walk with murderers."

Vlad bolted for the door and down the stairs. He kept expecting Mr. Otis to follow him, but by the time he reached the hospital, he was sure Otis wasn't there.

He caught Nelly at the nurses' desk and immediately launched into a quietly hysterical explanation of his presence. "Mr. Otis knows I'm a vampire and he's a vampire too and he killed Mom and Dad, not to mention Mr. Craig, so we have to get out of here! Do you think we could fly somewhere? Maybe the Bahamas? Or Australia? I'm thinking somewhere sunny."

Nelly listened intently before picking up her sweater and whispering something to one of the other nurses. She ushered him out the door and took a deep breath before speaking. "Now calm down, Vladimir. You seem awfully upset. Let's start with Mr. Otis knowing your secret."

They walked down the street, toward their house, and Vlad started to explain. He reiterated everything he'd told her the night of the dinner, but this time showed her the note Mr. Otis had scribbled on his essay. When he was finished, Nelly looked more concerned than fearful for their lives. "Where's Mr. Otis now? I should have a word with him, set him straight. That's a strange thing to accuse somebody of without any proof, being a vampire. Don't you think?" She gave him a sidelong look, and Vlad shrugged.

They continued walking toward their house. The silence broke when Nelly said, "We'll just straighten this out right now, Vlad. No worries."

Vlad jerked his eyes toward the house. Mr. Otis stood in

the front yard, near the porch. Vlad squeezed his aunt's arm and halted his steps, but Nelly tugged him along, as if his fears were unreasonable. She smiled at Mr. Otis, but Otis didn't smile back. "Mr. Otis, may we have a word? It seems Vlad is upset by something you wrote on his paper."

Mr. Otis had his eyes locked on Vlad. His skin was pale, his jaw set. His eyes had sunk in some, as if he needed either rest or sustenance—or both. He nodded slowly and gestured to the door, as if by retaining his gentlemanly qualities, his crimes would be ignored.

Vlad pulled away from Nelly, remaining with his feet firmly fixed to the sidewalk.

Nelly cast him with a sympathetic glance. "Come inside, Vladimir. Let's all talk this out. You'll feel better after we do, I promise."

Otis stepped closer, but despite his fears, Vlad didn't back away. "Yes, Vladimir, let's go inside. We wouldn't want your secrets becoming public now, would we?"

Vlad didn't say a word. In his mind, the image of those words on his paper, the image of Otis's hat in Mr. Craig's house, the image of his parents' bodies reduced to ashes flipped over and over, like a sick Rolodex of morbid thoughts.

Nelly retreated into the house, probably hoping Vlad would give up and follow. He resisted doing just that until Otis walked inside and closed the door. When Vlad entered, he heard Otis's voice in the living room. "No more running. No more giving your ward the opportunity to hear me out. You'll both listen now, and then I can deal with what must be done."

Vlad peeked around the corner. Nelly was sitting on the couch and Otis was pacing in front of her. Vlad's aunt looked spellbound.

Otis tilted his head toward a chair. "Sit down, Vladimir."

Vlad looked over his shoulder at the door and then at the stairs. He could get out, get help, bring the cops back, and explain that Otis was a madman. But Otis would kill Nelly for sure and divulge to the world that Vlad was a vampire. Loathe the idea of listening to the fiend as Vlad did, he knew when he was trapped. He sat in the chair and watched Otis pace silently for several minutes.

"Where's the book?" Mr. Otis was looming over him, and though the room was warm, Vlad swore he could see clouds of breath escaping from his teacher's mouth. Vlad glanced at the leather-bound book, which was lying on the coffee table where he'd left it. Otis followed his gaze and, in a few steps, snapped the book up in his hands. "How much of this have you read?"

Vlad shook his head, professing ignorance of the book's contents. "I haven't read a word. It's written in some weird language." He shrugged and offered, "I'm not even sure it *is* a language."

Mr. Otis blinked and then blinked again. He looked at the book in his hands and back at Vlad. Clutching the book to his chest, he resumed his pacing across the room. "Your father never taught you Elysian code? The vampiric language?" he asked.

Vlad pursed his lips stubbornly. "How did you know my father?"

Mr. Otis's booming voice reverberated in the room. "Did he teach you the code?"

"I have no idea what you're talking about." Vlad looked at Nelly, who shook her head, indicating she was clueless as well. It didn't surprise him that she was. His dad had been pretty secretive about the vampire world—apparently *very* secretive. He dropped his eyes to the book in Mr. Otis's hands.

Mr. Otis loosened his grip on the book. "So you don't know." He lowered his voice so that Vlad had to strain to hear him. "Did Tomas ever speak of Elysia? The vampire world?"

Vlad shot Mr. Otis a glare, and suddenly a wave of hunger washed over him. He could see himself biting into his teacher's neck, popping the skin between his teeth like a berry until the juices flowed down his throat and filled his belly. He wanted to taste Mr. Otis's blood, and he was starting not to care that he'd be injuring another person. He squeezed his eyes shut and then opened them again, once more under control. Mr. Otis might be a monster, but Vlad was nothing like him. "Why are you asking me so many questions? I don't know anything. Just let us go." He glared again, but Mr. Otis was no longer looking at him.

Mr. Otis's eyes were kind of glazed, and he was regarding the space between Vlad's feet with growing interest. "I can see it in your thoughts, like watching a short film. He told you about Elysia, but as bedtime stories, fairy tales. And he told you so little. He left out most of it, even the name, leaving you with false images embedded in your imagination."

Otis shook his head, raising his gaze to meet Vlad's. "The journal."

Otis stretched his mouth wide, exposing his fangs and eliciting a gasp from Nelly. "Your father was an outlaw, Vlad. He left Elysia for the love of your mother. Revealing vampiric heritage to humans is forbidden, let alone engaging in a romance with one. Those who do are hunted down, and their lives are taken for their crimes."

Though he fought it, a tear dripped from the corner of Vlad's eye and rolled down his cheek. He didn't want to cry. Not here in front of his parents' murderer, not here when he was about to die. He tried to look away from Otis's fangs, but they gleamed in the soft light, demanding to be seen. Beside him, Nelly was shaking in her seat, muttering things that Vlad couldn't understand. He met Mr. Otis's eyes. "So that's why you killed my parents. But why did you kill Mr. Craig? And why kill us? We haven't broken any of your laws."

Mr. Otis stopped, as if Vlad had kicked him hard in the chest. "Is that what you think? No, Vlad. I could never . . . I wouldn't kill you. I could never bring myself to harm a family member." Otis's fangs shrank slightly. He regarded Vlad with shimmering eyes. "Vladimir, I'm Tomas's half brother. Your uncle."

"What?" Vlad blinked again, trying to make some kind of sense out of the words his teacher had spoken, but he couldn't. What Mr. Otis had said was crazy.

Nelly glanced nervously between Vlad and Mr. Otis.

"My uncle?" Vlad said. "But you killed my parents and Mr. Craig."

"I most certainly did not."

"Then for glob's sake, why'd you scare us like that?" said Aunt Nelly. It was something she had always said as long as Vlad had known her: *for glob's sake*. Vlad rolled his eyes, then looked to Mr. Otis for his reply.

Mr. Otis looked at Nelly and then at Vlad, stretching out his palms in front of him as if he were pleading for forgiveness. "I'm sorry. It wasn't my intent to frighten you. I needed you to sit and listen. Every time I tried to talk to you, you'd run away. I need you to tell me what you know about Tomas and Mellina, and exactly what happened to both of them."

He glanced out the window again and then took a seat on the sofa, his elbows on his knees, his fingers raking back the hair from his face. "I was shocked to hear of their deaths. In fact, after Mr. Craig disappeared, I volunteered to take his teaching spot to find you, Vlad. I thought if I found you, I could find Tomas. I'd never planned to harm you or your parents. I only hoped to protect you from the vengeful justice of Elysia."

Tears coated his cheeks, and the sight of them made Vlad feel insignificant and small. The man he'd thought a monster was braver than he was. Brave enough to cry.

Nelly stood and crossed the room, placing a caring hand on Mr. Otis's shoulder. "We don't know what happened. It was an accident, their death. A dark mystery to us all."

Vlad swallowed a lump in his throat and pushed the image of his parents to the back of his mind. "Where is Elysia?"

A sigh escaped Otis. "All around you. Elysia isn't a place one can visit, Vlad. It's what we call vampire society. Coexisting with our own world—that is Elysia. The council gathers in Stokerton." He tapped the book's cover and handed it back to Vlad. "Everything you need to know is in here. I can teach you the code if you'd like. But later, when things are safer for you." His eyes shifted to the door, as if something terrible were going to burst through it at any second.

Vlad gripped the book in both hands. A million questions cluttered his mind. "But your hat ... and that symbol ..."

"I need you to trust me, Vladimir. I loved your father. We were more than brothers, we were best friends. It pained me when he left, when he chose your mother over Elysia, but it was his choice to make and I respected that."

He pulled up his sleeve and held his wrist up for them to see. Vlad cringed a bit at the symbol—a guilty cringe, one from a boy who'd actually accused his uncle of being a murderer. When Otis turned his wrist, the symbol glowed slightly, like the glyph he and Henry had discovered in his father's study, like the one on the book he was holding.

"This is my symbol, my name in Elysian code. When a vampire vows to protect someone, we leave our symbol on something that belongs to them. It's called 'marking' and it serves as a warning to others that should they harm this person, they should expect harm returned to them by the one who did the marking. Vampires are honor-bound. If we bother to mark someone, it is taken quite seriously. Your father marked Mr. Craig as a vow to protect him, by carving his name on his porch, just as surely as I marked you by carving mine on the box in your dresser. Unfortunately, someone ignored your father's mark."

"Who *did* kill Mr. Craig?" Nelly blurted.

"D'Ablo, though I'm not sure why. He could have fed on any number of Bathory citizens—did, in fact, on a young woman. But why he chose a man who'd been marked by your father is beyond me. Perhaps he'd hoped to anger Tomas, bring him out of hiding, which is where all of Elysia believes him to be."

Otis went to the window and pulled the drapes open an inch. It was already dark outside and there was strange electricity in the air, as if a storm was fast approaching.

"Who is D'Ablo, anyway?" Vlad asked.

The normally mellow Amenti jumped at the glass, hissing at the shadowy figure that was approaching the gate. Vlad jumped too and tried to see out the window. His heart was racing.

"That's D'Ablo," Otis said. "The president of the Elysian council. You remember him, Vlad. He was the one I was talking to while you were in the tree the other night."

Vlad blushed at the realization he'd been caught. Nelly muttered something that sounded very much like "grounded."

Otis pulled the drapes closed and turned from the window. "We need to hide you. D'Ablo has plans to take you to Elysia to be punished for your father's crimes—for your very existence."

Vlad's heart skipped a beat, and then continued its race. "I can hide in the attic."

"I'll come with you," Otis said. "D'Ablo mustn't see me."

They rushed up the stairs to the attic, shutting the door behind them. Otis sat on the attic floor and closed his eyes.

"What about Nelly?" Vlad asked.

"Shh. I'm trying to concentrate, Vlad."

"But she's still downstairs." Otis kept his eyes closed. He didn't answer, so Vlad could only guess his concerns were being ignored. Stretching his thoughts downstairs, he pushed into Nelly's mind, but found only a haze of images and general confusion.

Coming back to himself, Vlad looked at Otis. "Are you clouding her thoughts?"

Otis frowned in irritation. "I'm making her believe she knows nothing about you or me—it'll protect her from D'Ablo. Now hush."

Suddenly Otis opened his eyes wide and looked at Vlad. "He's taken her."

The meaning of his words hadn't settled in Vlad's mind before Otis was down the stairs and running toward the front door. Vlad bolted after him, calling to his aunt. When he reached the door, he found Otis slumped against the door-jamb, looking out into the darkness. Vlad swallowed hard. "Where is she?"

"He's taken her to Elysia, no doubt as bait for you."

As the anger boiled up within him, Vlad felt his fangs tear through the gums, pushing out to full length in a matter of seconds. He looked past Otis to the darkness outside. His heart rammed up against his ribs. "Come on." He shouldered past Otis and moved down the sidewalk, his eyes scanning the horizon for any sign of D'Ablo and Nelly.

Otis approached and placed a calm hand on his shoulder. "Where do you think you're going?"

"To Elysia. We're going to save my aunt."

A look of terrible concern crossed Otis's face. "Vladimir, that's exactly what he wants."

Vlad looked out into the night, determination in his eyes. "Then let's give it to him."

14
ELYSIA

OTIS SMIRKED, BUT WITH a glare from Vlad, he stopped. "If you're serious, we'll go. Have you mastered your ani-morphing capabilities yet?"

The young vampire answered this question the only way he could. With a blank stare.

Otis sighed. "Okay, so flying's out. We'll have to drive, but we'll need a drudge to watch the car. Do you have one?"

Vlad blinked again, and in his confusion, his fangs began to shrink. "A what?"

"A drudge." Otis waited for a spark of recognition in Vlad's eyes, but when he didn't see it, he sighed again in frustration. "Do you have a human who you can control? Who you can make do your bidding, follow your will with little effort?"

Vlad bit his bottom lip, not realizing his fangs were still protruding some, and licked away the blood quickly. "Well, I guess that would be Henry." He was pretty sure Henry wouldn't be amused at being referred to as a vampire's human slave, but he was the first person who came to mind. Vlad scratched his head and his fangs retreated fully. "But he doesn't really do everything I ask him to."

Otis raised an eyebrow. "Do you ask him or do you tell him?"

Vlad blinked, wondering just what Otis was driving at. "He's my friend. I ask him."

"Next time, tell him. Drudges have no will to resist their masters. Call him now. Tell him to meet us at my car in an hour." Otis looked determined, almost hungry. The sight of it gave Vlad a shiver.

"Why can't we leave now?"

Otis turned and walked down the sidewalk, and Vlad had to jog a bit to catch up. "Because we've got to feed."

Vlad slowed his steps. "The freezer's stocked. Where are you going?" He knew the answer, but didn't want to hear it.

Otis stopped walking and looked at him as if he was the dumbest kid alive. "To look for a human. We need to feed, Vlad."

"On a . . . *person?*" Vlad's stomach lurched as the last word passed over his tongue. It was all he could do to keep from puking. Blood was tasty, but these were his neighbors. And just think of the looks he might get at the next block party if he got caught. Pointing, accompanied by frantic whispers. *Isn't that the kid who ate Billy?*

No way.

"You act like you've never done this before."

"I haven't." Vlad looked down at the hole in his shoe. He felt embarrassed, but he wasn't sure why.

Otis seemed to be weighing his options as he watched a woman in a powder blue jogging suit trot by. He looked back at Vlad and then at the woman once again. "You've never fed on blood from its source?"

Vlad thought about telling Otis about Henry, but decided against it. "I've only ever had blood from a bottle or bag."

Otis's eyes widened in astonishment. "So your parents . . ."

"Dad was insistent that we live as normally as possible."

"That's not normal, Vlad." Otis gave his shoulder a gentle squeeze. "No vampire should live that way, and I doubt that your father followed his own rule. The hunger is undeniable. Eventually, you will feed on a person. You can't stop it."

Vlad stepped back, leaving Otis with his empty hand extended and a look of surprise on his face. Otis might be an experienced, worldly vampire, but he had no right to presume to know what had gone on with Tomas once he had left Elysia. Tomas had lived on blood bags and snack packs. Vlad knew. He'd seen.

Vlad narrowed his eyes. "Watch me," he told Otis. He turned and walked back to the house. At first, he didn't hear Otis behind him, and he half expected that Otis would run off after the jogger, but then his footsteps were echoing Vlad's. Vlad smiled triumphantly. They'd dine on bagged blood.

▼ ▼ ▼

An hour after Vlad rang Henry on his cell phone, Henry walked up to the open front door and greeted Vlad with a concerned glance. "What's going on? Why's Mr. Otis in your driveway?"

Otis was placing Vlad's backpack, full of blood bags he'd insisted they'd need, into the back of his car. He looked up at Henry. "Come here, drudge. Help me get the car ready, and we'll get going."

Vlad cringed.

Henry threw Vlad a glance. "What did he just call me?"

"Never mind. I'll explain everything later. Just go help him, will you? Somebody took my aunt. We've gotta go save her." Henry nodded. There were questions in his eyes, but he ran over and helped Otis with the car.

Vlad smirked. Maybe there was something to this drudge thing after all. He *had* noticed that his schoolbooks seemed to be getting heavier as the years went on ... plus, there were the mounds of homework to consider.

They piled into the car—Henry in the back, Vlad in the front, Otis in the driver's seat. As they started out of town, Vlad looked at Otis and cleared his throat. "So ... you came to Bathory to protect my father, not to bring him back to Elysia?"

Otis gave Vlad a brief smile, then focused again on the road. "Yes, Vlad. The council supported my efforts, as I'm likely the only person your father would have surrendered to. Of course they didn't know I came to warn him, not ensnare him."

"How do we get there?" Vlad asked. "To Elysia, I mean." To his amazement, he could already hear Henry snoring in the backseat. That guy could fall asleep on a car trip to the mailbox.

The dashboard lights cast a cool blue on Otis's face. He was watching the road intently. "Have you noticed that history books make no mention of whose idea it was to build cities, Vlad? They theorize, yes, and place the Egyptians, Greeks, and Romans at the center of their theories, but historians really don't know who came up with the design for metropolitan areas. Not human historians, anyway."

Vlad raised an eyebrow. "Are you saying vampires invented cities?"

"Quite. What better place for a superior race to hide than at the heart of an enormous population, where buildings are always busy despite the time of day, where large numbers of people live in a relatively small area, and a dead body is discounted as just another victim?" He smiled, obviously proud of his heritage—of *their* heritage. "We also invented Latin, chess, and PlayStation."

Vlad shifted in his seat. He could believe Otis's story about old stuff like Latin and chess, but PlayStation? *Puh-lease.* "I thought that was Sony's idea."

"Who do you think runs Sony?" Otis raised a sly eyebrow

at him in the darkness, and Vlad laughed despite the tension in his bones.

Vlad leaned against the door and dozed until the car came to a stop in front of a thirteen-story office building in downtown Stokerton—about an hour north of Bathory. He rubbed his eyes and reached back, smacking the still-snoring Henry on the knee. Otis opened the glove box and pulled out a small squirt gun. He held it out to Henry, a look of genuine terror in his eyes. "This is pure garlic juice. If anyone comes near the car, squirt them. Don't listen for explanations or let them get close to you. Just squirt them and then roll the window up. Keep the doors locked until you see either me, Nelly, or Vladimir." He started to open his door, then he looked at Henry again. "And don't squirt Vlad or me. It would mean an extremely painful wound, and if it managed to seep into our mouths or an open cut, it would mean death. Be extremely careful, drudge."

After Otis got out of the car, Henry grabbed Vlad by the sleeve. "Why does he keep calling me that?"

Vlad sighed. This was not a conversation he wanted to have while who knows what was happening to his aunt. "I'll tell you later. Right now just sit here and watch out for anybody who looks suspicious, okay?"

Henry nodded and settled back in his seat, the small squirt gun clutched against his chest. He looked like a *Romper Room* Rambo, waiting to take on the world.

Vlad got out and followed Otis to the revolving doors. "Won't they know we're coming if we use the front door?"

"They already know we're here, Vlad." Otis stepped through the door with a glance behind him at the car.

Vlad had never felt so scared in his life.

The elevator smelled like a weird mixture of cinnamon buns and moldy carpet. An older gentleman and a woman in a dark blue business suit with her hair in a tight bun entered after Vlad and Otis. Otis merely smiled at them as he glanced at the panel of numbered buttons. The elevator shifted, carrying them up several floors before it stopped and the man exited. Otis leaned past the woman with a flirtatious glance that said, "Allow me." Hidden in the wood next to the panel was a glyph, which he touched, inciting it to glow brightly.

Otis's eyes didn't change colors.

The panel of buttons slid down, revealing another set of buttons. Otis pressed LOBBY and the woman pressed 4. The elevator began its descent, and when they reached the fourth floor, the strange woman got out without a word. Otis leaned back on the handrail. "Not what you expected, is it?"

"I was thinking something with bats and an ominous moon floating above."

Otis raised his eyebrows and chuckled. The elevator door opened onto a posh lobby with a well-polished marble floor, black leather sofas, and a large grandfather clock against the far wall. Vlad followed Otis to the front desk, and after Otis had a brief, mumbled conversation with the receptionist, they settled on one of the sofas and waited—for what, Vlad couldn't be sure. The Muzak version of "Who Let the Dogs Out?" was pouring out of unseen speakers around them. Vlad rubbed his temples, trying to block out the sound. "Doesn't this strike you as a bit too corporate?"

Otis folded his hands in his lap and tilted his head to the side. "What do you mean?"

Vlad flashed him an incredulous look, but Otis didn't react to it. "I mean doesn't it seem just a little bit strange that we whisk off in the night to a world where vampires are the norm, only to end up in an office lobby drumming our fingers?" Otis blinked at him, clearly not getting Vlad's point. Vlad sank in his seat and crossed his arms in front of him. "Never mind. It's just weird, is all."

"I think you've seen too many movies, Vlad."

The curvaceous redhead behind the desk stood and nodded to Otis. "Mr. Otis, you can go in now." She sat down again, but not before giving Vlad a wink.

Otis stood and brushed invisible dust from his slacks before gesturing to the large double doors to the left of the receptionist's desk. "Shall we, Vlad?"

Vlad was quite sure they shouldn't, but he stood anyway and walked through the double doors.

Behind the doors was a significantly darker, more appropriately ominous room. Large silk rugs covered the floor and tall, thin windows marked their passage across the length of the room, toward the table at the other end. Six men and three women sat facing the door, with nothing but the polished black table between them and Vlad. Behind them was an oversize, glossy black fireplace.

Otis grabbed Vlad's arm and pulled him toward the gathered group. His fingers pressed brutally into Vlad's skin as he flung Vlad forward.

Vlad stumbled and fell to the floor. He flashed Otis a confused glance.

Otis straightened his shoulders proudly. "As requested, council, I've brought you the son of Tomas Tod."

The tall vampire at the center met Vlad's eyes. Vlad instantly recognized him as the man in black. D'Ablo, Otis had called him. "We are indeed grateful for your efforts, Otis. Even though the results took what seemed like ages to come by."

"My apologies, Mr. President. It took longer than expected to locate the boy. And I had to be certain he was Tomas's son before bringing him in. I'd hoped to locate Tomas first, to please the council with an unexpected end to our hunt, but the boy is clever." Otis dropped his eyes to Vlad and shook his head. "Too much like his father. I fear locating Tomas will take even longer."

Vlad looked up at Otis, frozen to his spot on the floor. What was Otis talking about? Tomas was dead. He knew that.

D'Ablo slid a small stack of papers toward one of the women, who began scribbling notes on each sheet. "We'll find

Tomas soon enough. Quite soon, I'd wager, with the boy's assistance."

Vlad parted his lips to speak, but only an inaudible whisper escaped him. "But my dad is dead."

D'Ablo offered Otis a nod. "You've done well. As reward, see to the lad's guardian. We have no further need of her, this"—he glanced at one of the papers in front of him—"Nelly."

Vlad got to his feet. His legs felt like Jell-O. He cast another glance at his uncle, this one full of trepidation. "Otis?"

But Otis wasn't looking at him. His eyes were fixed on D'Ablo.

Vlad watched in horror as the corners of Otis's mouth lifted in a smile.

Vlad grabbed Otis's sleeve, but was shaken off. "What? No! You're my uncle! You're supposed to help me!"

Arms appeared from nowhere and grabbed Vlad's shoulders, holding him still.

Otis turned back to the double doors without so much as a glance at Vlad.

Vlad fought against the guards as hard as he could. He wrenched his shoulders away, but the guards grabbed his arms and picked him up off the floor. Vlad's eyes flashed in hatred and his fangs nearly jumped from his gums. "Otis! What's wrong with you? How could you do this?"

The cry caused Otis to pause. He turned to Vlad and moved closer, his lip curled in a snarl. "Vladimir, how could I not? This is my home, my family. You ... were nothing more than a mistake my brother made."

Hot tears streamed down Vlad's cheeks. He lowered his voice, hoping that the man he'd thought Otis was, the man he wanted very much for him to be, would hear him and end this madness. "Don't hurt her, Otis. Don't hurt Nelly."

Otis parted his lips, revealing shimmering fangs, and turned back to the door. In ten steps, he was gone: a betrayer about to turn murderer.

D'Ablo cleared his throat. "Vladimir Tod ... I've been looking for you for a long time. You're not an easy person to find. But I imagine you're well aware of that."

Vlad's chest shook with every beat of his heart. He stared at the door, willing Otis to return and make things right again. But the doorknob stayed horrifically still.

"Especially when you're being helped. Now ... who has been assisting you in hiding from Elysia, young one?"

Vlad dried his tears on his sleeve. He needed time—time to figure out what he was going to do. When he spoke, his voice cracked. "No one. And I wasn't hiding. I didn't even know you guys existed until recently."

D'Ablo shook his head slowly in disbelief, a smirk on his lips. "Surely you knew there were other vampires."

Vlad counted the vampires. There were thirteen, including the guards. He might be able to wriggle away from the two that were holding him and outrun the rest. But what then? The most his flitting mind could think of involved scenarios not so unlike the *Scooby-Doo* mysteries. "No. I didn't. Up until a few weeks ago, I thought I was the only one left."

D'Ablo rounded the table. He clutched Vlad's jaw with his gloved hand, examining his face intently. "You look as I expect your father looked when he was a boy. Same eyes... hair...yes. I suspect you'd age to look strikingly similar to Tomas."

D'Ablo turned back to the table, his voice deep and clear. "If left unpunished, you would surely follow in your father's crime-shadowed footsteps."

Vlad shook his head. "Punished? But I haven't done anything."

D'Ablo's eyes flashed in irritation. "Your father is an ingenious man, young Vladimir, having successfully remained hidden from this council for some fourteen years. Give us his location and you may live. Where is Tomas Tod?"

Vlad pressed his lips together, refusing to meet his questioner's gaze. Inside his head he felt a gentle nudge and relaxed his mouth.

The vampire asked again, his voice smooth and coaxing. "Where is Tomas Tod?"

Vlad could hear another sound in the room. It resembled his voice so closely, but he couldn't recall having parted his lips to speak. Still, the voice said, "He's dead."

The vampire nodded before conferring quietly with his peers. Coming to some sort of conclusion marked by nods and mumbles, the council collectively waved Vlad away. The

guards squeezed his arms tightly and pulled him toward another set of double doors. Vlad felt the temporary calm that
had washed over him rinse away and struggled against the
guards' strong grip. "Where are you taking me?"

The double doors opened to reveal Otis. His collar was
torn, and his tongue darted out to lap at the blood on his lip.
Vlad recoiled in horror. "You killed her. You monster—you
killed Nelly."

Vlad kicked forward, throwing the guards off balance. In an
instant, he was free and running at Otis with his fist raised.

Otis closed his hand quickly over Vlad's wrist and spun
him around, stopping the attack. He held Vlad still and spoke
in a chilling tone, his lips only inches from Vlad's ear. "Now,
Vladimir. You wouldn't hurt your uncle, would you?"

D'Ablo smiled and made a note on one of the papers on
the table. "Take young Vladimir to the stockade. Deal with
him as we discussed earlier, Otis."

Otis grabbed Vlad by the collar, but Vlad didn't fight him.
He was too tired, too sad, and too overwhelmed by the events
of the day to fight. All he wanted was to be back at home,
munching on some of Nelly's chocolate-chip cookies and playing video games with Henry.

Henry. What would become of him now? He imagined
Otis would kill him. The spray he'd handed Henry wasn't garlic at all. It was likely just water, and poor Henry had been
duped as well. Because of Vlad, those closest to him would be
made to suffer.

Otis led him down a long, dark hallway. Near the end were three cells with bars like those Vlad had seen on the cop shows Nelly watched on Thursday nights. But there would be no more cop shows for Nelly, no more late-night talks, no more snack packs or tea. There would be no more hugs that he pretended to loathe, no conversations he faked being bored with.

No more Nelly.

Otis slid open the door to the cell and nudged Vlad inside.

The floor of the cell was covered in yellow hay, as if the area were intended for livestock. Vlad shivered, picturing Nelly in the small space.

Otis slid the door closed, locking them in the cell together. He circled the room, surveying the floor and the walls. He turned to Vlad, a look of hunger on his face. His voice was no more than a rough whisper. "You have no idea what's going on here, Vladimir."

"No. I think I do." The tears threatened to return, but Vlad cursed them and tried hard to steady his shaking hands.

Otis had begun pacing back and forth, like an animal ready to attack. "I know what it must look like, but things had to go this way. I had no choice."

"You have a choice now. Don't kill me, Otis." Vlad met Otis's eyes. "Please."

Otis grabbed Vlad by the shoulder and shook him once, hard. "Don't you understand? If the council wants you dead, they won't stop until they know that you are. There is only one way for either of us to get out of here alive."

Vlad shuddered, realizing that his words were in vain. There was no way to talk his uncle out of doing what he had planned to do from the beginning. He dropped his eyes to the ground. He wasn't about to let Otis see him cry again.

In the corner of the cell was a square metal plate set into the floor. Caught on its edge was a single scrap of fabric. The pattern matched the shirt Nelly had been wearing when Vlad had last seen her. Despite his bitter anger toward Otis, Vlad pointed to the plate. "What's that?"

"It's a disposal chute. After prisoners are ... dealt with, their bodies are deposited in there. It leads to the incinerator." A look of shame washed over him.

Vlad straightened his shoulders. The floor at his feet was dotted with fresh blood—Nelly's blood. The thought of it made him retch. "How could you, Otis? How could you do that to Nelly? How can you do it to me?"

The color bled from Otis's face. He lifted Vlad's backpack and unzipped it, revealing the bags of blood inside. Three of the bags were empty. Otis's face was blank as he pointed to the floor. "That isn't Nelly's blood. Vladimir, I'm on your side."

Vlad blinked. "I'm getting really tired of these guessing games, Otis. What exactly is going on here?"

Otis lowered his voice and stepped closer. Vlad tried not to budge, but he took a step back in spite of his intentions. Otis frowned. "Nelly is outside in the car. I came back for you. The blood was just to convince the rest of Elysia I'd killed her."

Vlad looked at the empty blood bags and then over his shoulder. "What about handing me over to those thugs? And saying those . . . those horrible things?"

Otis slipped two of the bags from Vlad's backpack and bit them open. He handed the backpack to Vlad and began squirting more blood onto the floor. "I apologize for that. It was merely a ruse to buy me enough time to save your aunt . . . and you."

"A ruse? They could have killed me!" Vlad slipped on the slick floor, but caught his balance before he fell. "What about Henry?"

Otis gave the bags a final squeeze before tossing them back into the backpack and zipping it closed. "He's fine. But we'd better hurry. D'Ablo doesn't trust me fully. That's why he came to Bathory to gather you himself." He crossed the room and lifted the big metal plate, casting Vlad an expectant glance. "Get in."

Vlad raised an eyebrow. "I don't think so. It seems D'Ablo and I have something in common. I don't trust you, either." He shrugged and slung the backpack over his shoulder. "Call me cynical."

"We don't really have time to discuss this right now." Otis climbed into the hole and slid down the chute.

Vlad didn't spend much time weighing his options. If he stayed, the vampires of Elysia would most certainly kill him.

Jumping into an incinerator after the madman who might have just killed his aunt wasn't much of a chance . . . but it was all Vlad had. He got on his knees and slid in feet first to follow his uncle. He wedged his sneakers against the side of the metal shaft and eased his way down, stopping himself before he ran into Otis, who was wedged several feet below him.

"Glad you could make it." Otis's voice, though hushed, echoed up to Vlad. "This way."

Otis lifted a small screen door and slipped inside. Vlad crawled through it after his uncle. They were in a ventilation shaft, and moving slowly, as Otis was barely able to squeeze through the opening. After several yards, the tunnel widened and the metal stopped, leaving Vlad crawling over dirt and rock.

The tunnel seemed to go on forever—at least that's what it felt like to Vlad, who was scooting along on his belly in the dark on a rough, rocky surface to who knows where. Otis was ahead of him by several feet. Neither spoke until Otis opened a round hatch at the end and moonlight poured into the small passage. "Tomas and I dug this tunnel before he left Elysia, back when he was vice president of the council."

Vlad slid out behind Otis, his feet once again on firm pavement. Otis was looking around for the car. "He was a good man, your father."

Henry was standing at the opening to an alley, waving his arms. Vlad ran toward him, and Henry looked over his shoulder at the nearby car. Nelly was leaning against it, looking scared and shaken, but alive. Vlad slowed as he passed Henry, who gave his arm a light punch, and approached Nelly with a relieved sigh. He couldn't bear losing Nelly—not after losing his parents. She was more than his guardian. She was his friend, his family. Nelly made everything all right, and if she were gone, nothing would ever be all right again. She managed a smile before he wrapped his arms around her. Vlad's chest grew heavy. His eyes welled with tears. He'd almost lost her. He'd almost been orphaned...again. Nelly kissed his brow repeatedly, and Vlad welcomed it. Silently he vowed that he would protect her from harm for as long as blood coursed through his veins.

Cold, quiet laughter filled the alley. "Well now, isn't this sweet?"

Vlad turned to see D'Ablo, who was backed by four large bodyguards. D'Ablo sneered. "Did you think it would be so easy to escape your father's past, boy? Did you think I was blind to Otis's feeble attempts to keep me from you?" He tossed off his black overcoat, and it fell to the pavement.

Otis glanced at Nelly, who ushered Henry into the car. She reached for Vlad's shoulder, but Vlad shook her off.

D'Ablo took a single step forward, his eyes locked with Vlad's.

Otis stepped between them. "We cannot hold the boy accountable for his father's crimes."

"It is I who lead this council, Otis. Therefore, I will decide his fate." D'Ablo nodded to one of his guards, and the man swaggered over and grabbed Otis by the arm.

Otis wriggled uselessly. His face reddened in anger. "I won't let you harm him!" Miraculously, Otis shoved the brute aside and broke into a run toward D'Ablo. Time slowed to a crawl as his feet slapped the pavement.

D'Ablo watched his approach with an amused glint in his eye. When Otis was merely feet from him, D'Ablo swung his arm and slapped Otis in the face with such force that Vlad thought he could hear the bones crack. Otis tumbled into the arms of the waiting bodyguards. They dropped him to the ground and pinned him.

Vlad was left to face D'Ablo alone.

Vlad looked from his wounded uncle to D'Ablo. His heart began a strong, steady pounding. D'Ablo's stern jaw relaxed some as he turned to face Vlad, and the corner of his mouth rose in a smirk. Vlad wondered if D'Ablo had been smirking when he'd killed his parents.

Vlad's mouth tightened. Tears threatened to well up in his eyes, but the sight of D'Ablo's clenching fists kept them at bay. Not only was Vlad facing his parents' killer—he was likely facing his own.

Vlad swallowed hard and straightened his shoulders, trying to look intimidating. His lower lip trembled slightly, betraying his fear. He swore and met D'Ablo's cold eyes.

D'Ablo smoothed his shiny black leather gloves onto his hands and smiled triumphantly. "Now, Vladimir, do you have any final words before I carry out your sentence?"

Vlad didn't move. He could barely breathe. But he'd spent most of his eighth-grade year running from bullies. He was tired of it. "My father wrote about Elysia. He said it was a place of brotherhood and camaraderie." Vlad slanted his eyes. "He never mentioned it was full of egotistical jerks in bad suits."

D'Ablo paused. His posture hadn't changed at all, but he was no longer smiling. His fangs gleamed in the moonlight. "Being raised away from Elysia has robbed you of an important lesson in respect and in fear, young Vladimir." He stepped closer.

D'Ablo couldn't have been more wrong—Vlad *was* afraid. With every step D'Ablo took, Vlad felt his heartbeat quicken. His pulse raced along with his thoughts. But he wasn't about to show D'Ablo his fear. If his dealings with Bill and Tom had taught him anything, it was this: never let them see you sweat. Vlad resisted the urge to flee and said, "Oh, give it up! Could you be more of a stereotype? You come out to a dark alley, dressed in black, surrounded by guys the size of Dumpsters— what are you going to do next, tell me that you *vant to suck my blood?* I only wish I'd brought my crucifix with me—we could end this whole thing right now." Vlad glanced around the alley. He needed a weapon, something to defend himself with long enough to get Otis, Nelly, and Henry and run.

D'Ablo snarled. He drew his hand back and it whistled through the air.

Vlad's cheek exploded with pain. The heels of his hands scraped the pavement as he fell to the ground.

D'Ablo looked pleased. "You'd better watch that sharp tongue of yours, child. Before I rip it from your skull."

Vlad reached up with shaking fingers and touched his cheek lightly. He spat a mouthful of blood on the ground and looked up at his attacker. "You're pathetic. If Elysia is full of guys like you, my dad was right to leave." He slipped his hands inside his front pockets. A stick of gum, a broken pencil . . . nothing remotely useful.

D'Ablo drew his leg back and kicked Vlad in the ribs. Hard.

Something cracked, and Vlad let out a scream.

D'Ablo was bent over him, so close that Vlad could feel the vampire's breath against his skin. "Will you run like your father, Vlad? Or will you stand and fight?"

Vlad clutched his torso and let out a sob. This was it, then. D'Ablo was going to kill him if he didn't do something soon. Slowly, he moved his hand to the back pockets of his jeans. Tears threatened to fall, but Vlad choked them back. His bruised cheek and injured rib seemed to throb in the same rhythm. In his head, he was repeating his mantra of "never let them see you sweat, never let them see you sweat," but what he said out loud, with a quaver in his voice, was, "What's the matter, D'Ablo? Do the other vampires pick on you? You feel a need to take it out on someone smaller than you, is that it?" He pulled a small object from his pocket and looked at it. It was the black cylinder he'd found in the attic.

D'Ablo's eyes widened. He took a step back.

Vlad looked from the smooth tube to D'Ablo. D'Ablo couldn't possibly be afraid of it. Could he? It was nothing, really, just a trinket that had belonged to Vlad's father. Probably about as dangerous as ChapStick. Still, Vlad was ready to utilize any tool he could. He held it out toward D'Ablo, who stepped back again—far enough that Vlad wondered where he was going. The men who were holding Otis down were exchanging terrified whispers.

"Where did you get that?" D'Ablo had stopped his retreat. He looked warily from Vlad to the object in his hand.

Vlad feigned both knowledge of the tool and the confidence that he could use it. "It was a gift from my father before he died."

The brutes had apparently reached the conclusion that D'Ablo wasn't worth dying for, as they released their hold on Otis and hurried back inside. Otis stood and brushed the grime of the alley from his clothes, but he didn't speak. And, Vlad noted with interest, Otis didn't move any closer.

D'Ablo forced a smile. "It's a fascinating instrument. May I have a closer look?"

Vlad pointed the tube at D'Ablo as he rose to his feet. His rib screamed and his voice shook. "Stay back!"

As if a light had gone on over his head, D'Ablo relaxed visibly. "Or you'll what, Vlad? A real vampire wouldn't point a Lucis at another without the full intention of using it. So are you merely threatening me until you can figure out how to use it, or do you understand the power that you now hold in your hands?" He stepped closer, his fangs long and fierce. Hunger flickered in his eyes.

Vlad tore his frightened gaze away from D'Ablo. His breaths came in shaken gasps. His fingers trembled against the cylinder. The end facing him bore the symbol that mirrored his father's tattoo, so like the symbol on the cover of the book.

D'Ablo broke into a sure stride. Saliva glistened on the tips of his exposed fangs.

Vlad pushed the sound of D'Ablo's approach out of his head. He thought of the book, of the panel at the back of his dad's suit closet. They'd both had the glyph. And when he'd touched it . . .

D'Ablo threw his head back and opened his mouth as wide as he could.

. . . when he'd touched it, the glyph had glowed. But not for Henry. It was a vampire shield—something to prevent humans from opening vampiric items. And if this thing had a glyph too . . .

D'Ablo lunged forward, spittle dripping from his mouth. A low, hungry, guttural cry left his lungs as he descended on Vlad.

. . . maybe, maybe . . .

Vlad looked at Otis, who nodded, understanding Vlad's thoughts without the use of telepathy.

Vlad ran his thumb across the glyph. It glowed brightly, and the cylinder shook in his hands. He held it tightly. A piercing white light shot from the opposite end, filling the alley with a blinding flash. Vlad squeezed his eyes shut and ran his thumb over the glyph once more. When he opened his eyes again, the light had faded—contained once more within the small black cylinder.

D'Ablo lay on the ground, clutching his stomach.

Well... clutching where his stomach should have been.

Through the enormous hole in D'Ablo's torso, Vlad could see the dark, moist pavement on the other side. D'Ablo looked up at him with flickering eyes and forced a laugh. "You think you've won? You think you've defeated me?"

Vlad tightened his grip on the tube, but stopped when Otis grabbed his arm. "It's over, Vlad. Leave him here to die."

Vlad knelt. His face was mere inches from D'Ablo's. "That was for Mr. Craig. And for anyone else you've ever hurt."

D'Ablo chuckled. Blood coated his lips. "Do you think it makes any difference, little one? There are thousands of vampires in the world, doing the same as I have."

Vlad held the Lucis up for D'Ablo to see. "Well, there's one fewer tonight."

D'Ablo coughed, sending a spatter of blood across Vlad's cheek, and then he was still.

On the drive home, as Henry snored beside him, Vlad allowed himself a few more tears: these for the father he knew so little about, and for the mother who'd never kiss him as Nelly had tonight, and for himself, because beneath the relief and general sense of well-being lurked something dark and disturbing—the knowledge that he would one day return to Elysia, that his father's journal would lead him there to seek answers to questions he had not yet asked.

Otis was driving, and Nelly was in the passenger seat. The soft blue light from the radio illuminated the front seat, giving Vlad a clear view of their profiles. They'd been talking for a short while—muttered voices that had softened into whispers. But now they were quiet. They were also holding hands.

Vlad pulled his backpack close and laid his head against the door. He was too riled up to sleep and had no idea how Henry could, so he stared out the window and counted stars as the lights of the city faded into blackness.

All that was ahead of him was the twinkle of starlight—and the comforting return home.

15
THE END OF A DARK JOURNEY

ENRY WAS SPRAWLED ACROSS the couch in Vlad's living room, already asleep. Vlad tossed an old afghan over him and joined Nelly and Otis in the dining room. Nelly looked weary, but relieved, and managed a smile. She pushed her teacup aside and got up from the table. "I'll be off to bed now, boys. My old bones just can't take the nightlife anymore." She kissed Vlad on the forehead, the way his mother used to. "Are you sure you're okay?"

"I told you, I'm fine." Vlad took a seat across from Otis. He winced as he sat, holding a hand to his injured rib. Nelly had given him and Otis pills for pain as soon as they got home, but Vlad's hadn't kicked in yet. But his rib would heal in a few days and the pain would be but a memory. Vlad glanced at the steaming blood in his cup, raised it to his lips, and drank.

Nelly nodded and retreated upstairs after a brief good night to Otis.

Otis placed his cup in the saucer and cleared his throat. He looked at Vlad. "I've been searching for you for years. It's been a real pleasure getting to know you, Vlad."

"Why does that sound like a good-bye?" He met Otis's eyes, the familiar feeling of loss already pricking his insides. "You can't just throw all this at me and then disappear. Besides, you're the only real family I've got."

Otis shook his head. "I wouldn't say that. Nelly is a wonderful guardian."

Vlad ran his finger thoughtfully over a knot in the wood of the table. Otis was right, of course, but it didn't stop Vlad from longing for something more concrete, for blood relations. Nelly was great, but she didn't know anything about being a vampire. "Why didn't you just tell me who you were when we first met?"

Otis managed a smile. "Because I wasn't sure if you were a vampire or not. Since you had a human mother, I couldn't be sure that you had inherited that part of your father's being. You're the first of your kind, Vlad. You're also remarkably gifted at blocking telepathy. I wasn't sure if it was your gift as a vampire or a charm Tomas had given you that blocked my telepathy. So I had to use other means to find out, such as the oral report and the essay—and the garlic."

"Oh, and thanks for that." Vlad dunked a cookie into his cup and took a bite. "I spend my whole life trying to hide what I am and you make me get up and tell the whole class." He gave Otis a grin. "Not awkward in the least."

Otis stretched his arms over his head and yawned. Outside, the sky was turning pink. It was almost dawn. "I needed to know where Tomas was so I could warn him that D'Ablo and the rest of Elysia had learned he was in Bathory. I couldn't reveal myself to you if you were human—that's a crime." Otis glanced out the window, looking a little concerned. From his jacket, he pulled out a small tube and proceeded to rub sunblock on his skin.

"But you told Nelly."

"Yes. And I would likely be punished for it if Elysia were to find out." Otis finished coating his exposed skin and put the tube back in his pocket.

Henry's snores drifted in from the living room. Then, after one loud snort, he was silent once again.

Vlad lowered his voice so as not to wake Henry. "When we were in Elysia, you mentioned that my dad had been vice president of that council."

"Yes. Well, that was a long time ago." Otis shifted in his seat, as if the sunrise were making him restless.

"So tell me about it." Vlad plucked another cookie from the plate on the table and nibbled.

Otis yawned again. Vlad resisted following suit. "Tomas had been on the council for more than a hundred years when I was turned from human into vampire, and for another three hundred before he left Elysia to raise you."

Vlad nearly choked on his cookie. "We live that long?"

"Most of us, yes." Otis drew his arms up around himself, as if the temperature had plummeted several degrees.

"Will I live that long?"

"I'm not sure, Vladimir. You're ... special." He shifted his eyes about the room, as if checking to make sure they were alone.

Vlad looked over his own shoulder for any unwanted presences. Otis's fidgeting was unsettling. "What do you mean?"

Otis sighed and pinched the bridge of his nose. "Vampires are made by sharing blood with a human and giving that human part of your essence. It's been this way since the beginning of time. But you ..." His Adam's apple bobbed as he swallowed hard. "Well, you were born this way, and that's extremely unusual. As I said before, you're the first of your kind."

Vlad cast Otis a worried glance. "Now that D'Ablo is gone, won't Elysia just send someone else to look for my father—and me?"

"No." Otis smiled at Vlad reassuringly. "I'm going to send word to the council that Tomas died in Bathory. And they now know you have the Lucis and are capable of using it. They won't come after you, Vlad."

"Otis ..." Vlad looked from his uncle to the hole in his shoe and back. "If D'Ablo didn't kill my parents, do you ... do you know who did?"

Otis was quiet for a moment, then met Vlad's eyes. "No, Vlad, I don't."

Vlad nodded. He was deeply disappointed, but not surprised. He wondered if he would ever know.

"Otis, will you"—he paused, trying to keep the doubt out of his voice—"will you teach me everything you can about being a vampire? There's no one else who can do it."

Otis's eyes sparkled warmly. "I would be honored to, Vlad."

Vlad cleared his throat. He didn't trust himself to speak.

Otis got up to check that Henry was still sleeping before turning back to Vlad. "When school is over, I'll return to Elysia and go into hiding. But I'll always return for you, whenever you need me."

Vlad hesitated, then blurted out, "What if I said I needed you now, that I need you to be around all the time?"

Otis was quiet for several minutes before rolling up his sleeve and exposing the tattoo on the inside of his wrist. It glowed slightly when he moved it closer to Vlad. "Do you remember when I told you about my mark—this symbol that, in the vampiric language, is my name? Well, it's also my tie to Elysia, to all of the vampiric brotherhood. Whenever I am scared or alone or saddened by events that I cannot control, I touch it and I'm reminded that I am part of something very special."

Vlad reached out slowly and brushed his fingers against the glyph. It brightened in response. A wave of sadness washed over him.

"The mark is normally given the day following a vampire's creation," Otis went on, "but as your beginning was one of a kind and you were nowhere near Elysia . . ."

"Just another thing I missed out on, huh?"

They exchanged sad smiles. Otis moved to leave, then turned back to Vlad. "It would be my great honor to give you your own mark, Vladimir. Of course, if you're not interested, I completely under—"

"I'd like that. I mean, it would mean a lot to me." Vlad tried hard to keep his eyes dry, but they brimmed with tears despite his efforts. "Will it hurt?"

"A bit. But a mark of your own will open worlds to you that you did not know existed." Otis smiled.

Vlad bit his bottom lip and nodded slowly. "Okay."

Otis reached for Vlad's wrist and gently pushed up his sleeve. Vlad watched as his uncle's pearl-white fangs elongated and slipped easily into his wrist. At first Vlad tensed as the teeth punctured him, then he began to feel weary, strangely dizzy. Otis's grip on Vlad's arm tightened, and Vlad felt a sudden surge of energy through his veins, like liquid fire. It was strange—he could feel Otis there, in his veins, in his blood, burning his energies into Vlad, and suddenly Vlad understood what it was to belong to Elysia. That by sharing space with any other of his kind, he was part of something bigger—that he was a vampire, a part of an ages-old family that would never leave him. He would never again be truly alone.

Otis pulled his mouth away, then helped to steady Vlad.

"Watch, Vladimir. Your mark is forming." Otis held Vlad's arm gently.

Vlad grew a little weak at the sight of blood on his open wrist, but marveled as the skin began to heal and the blood seeped back into his flesh, leaving behind a strange, glowing scar that darkened until Vlad's own tattoo had been created from within him. It was small, about the size of a fifty-cent piece, and looked just like Otis's mark, but for the two vertical lines inside the parentheses. When Otis released his arm, the mark dimmed some. Vlad whispered, "Thank you." He wanted to say more, but the words wouldn't come.

Otis brushed a small tear from his eye and smiled. Then he walked to the front door and stepped outside.

Vlad stepped out after him, rubbing his wrist and feeling stronger already. "Uncle Otis? Promise you won't leave forever."

Otis turned back to him and slid his top hat on. "That's a promise. But you have to promise me something, too."

Vlad nodded.

"That you'll be on the lookout for others like us. D'Ablo had many friends." Otis checked his pocket for keys. Triumphant in his search, he offered Vlad a nod. "And I expect you to get an A on the spelling test next Friday."

Vlad rolled his eyes. Apparently saving your teacher's life wasn't enough. "Three quick questions." Vlad followed him down the sidewalk toward the car. "What do I do if Henry asks me to explain what a drudge is?"

"That's up to you—you tell him or you don't. But I rather think you should." He opened the car door and cast Vlad a weary smile. "What else?"

Vlad bit his bottom lip and looked at the ground, then back at Otis. "Why did D'Ablo hate my dad so much?"

"He didn't, Vlad. In fact, they were good friends. D'Ablo was merely doing what he thought was the right thing to do." Otis pulled the door closed. "That's all any of us can really do."

Vlad wrinkled his forehead, trying to recall the word he'd heard D'Ablo use to describe him. "And...what's a...Pravus?"

Otis looked at Vlad, his face grave. He searched the air around him for the right words, and when he found them, they came out with a croak. "Just an old vampire legend, Vlad, about a boy who was born a vampire. Pay it no mind." With the rev of the engine, he drove off, leaving Vlad standing at the end of the driveway.

The sky was bright pink and gold. Vlad watched Otis drive off into the sunrise, like some sort of vampire cowboy. It had been a long night. And he hadn't even finished his math homework.

Vlad stepped back into the house and closed the door quietly behind him. Henry was still sleeping on the couch. Nelly was no doubt nestled under her flowered comforter upstairs. Vlad climbed the stairs, and after pausing to stroke Amenti's fur, he slipped into his bedroom, where he was greeted by the framed smiles of his mom and dad and by his bed—the most welcoming sights he'd ever seen.

16

THE MARK OF A VAMPIRE

L
IKE A MAN WHO HAS wandered through shadowed forests,
seeking reprieve from their looming darkness and strange,
creaking, haunting sounds, only to collapse in relief at his first
glimpse of light, Vlad sat down heavily at his desk on his last
day in eighth grade and surveyed the class around him. He
wasn't exactly sure what the point of the last day of school
was supposed to be, other than easing the summer janitor's
duties by emptying the desks and lockers. Principal Snelgrove
ensured that this task was done by making it a requirement in
order to attend Freedom Fest—an afternoon that began with
the final game of the Bathory Bats, the high school's much-
celebrated baseball team, and ended with the last dance of
the year in the school gym.

It should have been a happy day for Vlad. After all, he was
finally leaving junior high, and next year was full of possibilities. Bill and Tom would be freshmen, too, and have to deal

with bullies of their own. He and Henry would be high schoolers, and life would begin anew. But overshadowing what should have been a pleasant day was the knowledge that tonight Otis would be leaving, and though he'd reassured Vlad several times that he would return, his words hadn't lifted the deep, heavy, hollow feeling in Vlad's chest.

A flash of pink caught Vlad's eye. Meredith was wearing a pretty pink sundress. Vlad managed a smile, and to his delight, she smiled back, her cheeks blushing before she looked away. Vlad looked away, too, but only long enough to glimpse the tattooed symbol on the inside of his wrist. Feeling a surge of confidence, he straightened in his seat, returning his gaze to Meredith once again. "Hey, Meredith."

She looked at him, her blue eyes twinkling, and when she smiled again, Vlad felt like he was flying. "Hey, Vlad. How are you?"

"I'm great." He cleared his throat and glanced around before meeting her eyes. "But I'd be better if you went to the Freedom Fest dance with me."

Her lips parted, a glimpse of white porcelain as her smile spread into a grin. "I'd love to."

Vlad's heart drummed out an elated beat, and as he uttered the most ridiculous thing possible (*Did I just say thank you?* he asked himself), Mr. Otis entered the room, ushering in the final stragglers so they could get down to the business of their last day. "Good morning, class. I'm afraid I have bad news."

Otis dropped his bag on his chair and leaned against the desk. "After today, you are all finally free of my tyrannical grasp and now-infamous pop quizzes. Pressing matters are taking me away from the town of Bathory, despite much pleading on the part of the school board. So after the game this afternoon, I'll bid you all a fond farewell.

"But never fear. It may be my last day here ... but you are collectively beginning an exciting journey. I'm sure the coming years in Bathory High will prove far more fascinating than any one of my classroom hours." Otis smiled at his students, pausing for a moment with his eyes on Vlad.

Outside the open door stood Henry, most likely on his way to the final student council meeting of the year. He'd already been elected president of the ninth-grade student council beginning the following term, a big promotion from treasurer. He waved frantically at Vlad, who returned the favor. Henry held up a finger and turned his head for a moment. When he looked back at Vlad, he was wearing a pair of cheap plastic fangs and dancing around like such a dork that Vlad could no longer contain his laughter.

Mr. Otis looked at Vlad, then Henry. There was a silent pause before the door closed with a slam. Otis offered Vlad a wink. "Must be the wind."

Otis turned to the board and began scratching out details that needed to be addressed before the end of the day and the beginning of Freedom Fest.

Vlad leaned forward in his seat and pressed his cheek

against his palm. Out of the corner of his eye he could see his new tattoo glow slightly. Poking out of his backpack was his father's journal, carefully bookmarked where Vlad had left off reading. Beside it was a composition notebook.

Scribbled on the cover was *The Chronicles of Vladimir Tod.*